I0570493

Brewing Passion

INFUSION

LIZ CROWE

Infusion
ISBN # 978-1-78686-367-6
©Copyright Liz Crowe 2018
Cover Art by Posh Gosh ©Copyright August 2018
Interior text design by Claire Siemaszkiewicz
Totally Bound Publishing

Published in 2018 by Totally Bound Publishing, United Kingdom.

INFUSION

Dedication

This book is dedicated to my friend, fellow
Yogini, and personal inspiration,
Lora Rosenbaum, owner of Pure Hot Yoga in Ann
Arbor, Michigan.
We stayed in the room.

Chapter One

"*Forward motion. Don't think about it. Move. Put one foot in front of the other...*"

Gayle's hands hurt. She opened her eyes one at a time and saw why. She had her fingers wrapped around the thick leather-covered steering wheel so tight that when she released them with a wince, the expensive hand-stitching was embossed on her palm like a tattoo. She glanced out to see her fellow yogis unpacking their mats, towels and water bottles and heading toward the studio.

This had been a bad idea. She'd not planned to practice hot yoga today. She had an interview. A job interview. A crucial, life-altering dream-job interview with a major company that had recruited her via a top-secret headhunter. And yet here she sat, already sweaty, heart pounding, staring out into the parking lot and wishing she were anywhere but here.

But, of course, she needed this. Her hot yoga practice had been one of the few stable things in her life for the last year, two years — shit, almost three years now. It had been the only stable thing, if she were being completely honest. And one thing she prided herself on was total self-aware honesty.

She re-fastened her wilting ponytail and turned off the motor. The radio continued to drone sonorous news voices she no longer heard for the requisite thirty seconds before shutting down. Without the AC running, the interior of the car heated up fast in the midsummer sun.

But then again, she could be having some kind of shitty karmic early onset menopause, too. That would be exactly the thing, really. Even though she was only thirty-six going on thirty-seven. Her mother had gone through 'the change' at forty-five, after all. Tears burned behind her eyes, but she blinked them away.

There was no crying in hot yoga.

It was an iron-clad rule, at least for her.

With a teenager-worthy sigh, she hauled her yoga mat, towel and water bottle into her arms and stepped out onto the hot pavement. She'd done the calculations over and over in her head the night before. If she did this nine-thirty class, it put her home at eleven-forty. She only needed fifty minutes to get from shower to interview-ready and the damn thing wasn't until two o'clock. If she had an appetite, she could even eat some lunch in between since it was exactly twelve miles — which translated to about seventeen minutes travel — to the industrial park where she'd be meeting with the president of TriCities Distribution in hopes of convincing him that she wasn't overqualified for the sales director's job. She would give her eyeteeth to get the job. She'd even take less salary than he was offering — hell, she'd do it for ten dollars a day. She didn't need the money. She needed the distraction and she was damn good at selling beer and wine. Always had been.

She mentally reviewed the resume the headhunter had sent over to the company. The resume which had resulted in the company's president and CEO calling her within about an hour asking why in the world she'd consider working for his company—not that he didn't want her of course. It was just...

Gayle squeezed her eyes shut and tried to shut out the incessant buzz of memory. Today was not a time for lollygagging around in unhappiness. Today was a day of forward motion. And she was ready for it.

"Hey, girl," a voice called from her behind her. Gayle turned, a smile fixed on her face. She'd made a few new friends thanks to this yoga thing, most of them wealthy moms-from-home who had the hours between nine and two-thirty wide open for things like exercise, lunches, facials and whatnot. She'd been invited to some of the other activities but had demurred with random excuses for the past year or so. A period of time in which she had flopped around in sweats and no makeup for the first time in her adult life, wondering what to do next.

"Hi, Pam." She hoisted her mat and towel up under one arm so she could sip water from her yoga-studio-labeled stainless bottle. Her mouth was bone dry and she was already sweating—no wonder, since it was eighty-something degrees at nine-twenty a.m. She put the bottle to her lips and glanced over at the studio. A bank of windows in a long line of them, in a strip mall once abandoned by a large retailer then saved by another one plus a high-end grocery store.

"What's going on over there?" she asked, only half-interested.

The other woman shielded her eyes with one hand. "Window washers maybe?"

"Maybe," Gayle agreed. "Well, the sweat box awaits." She started across the hot tarmac, surprised when Pam grabbed her upper arm. "What?" They were not the sort of friends who touched each other. They were only fellow practitioner-sufferers. Pam was staring at what Gayle could now make out were two guys on top of a partially lifted platform. One of them was drilling something over his head. The other was sorting through a stack of the somethings piled on the platform.

"Lord, those guys are…hot." Pam's voice was a loud whisper. "Look!"

Gayle looked. She even made a show of taking off her Ray-Bans to see better, as if she cared. "Hmm…guess so. Well…" She glanced at the fingers still dug into her biceps. "Better get inside."

Pam's face flushed when she let go of Gayle's arm. Flustered, she recovered and treated Gayle to her bleached smile. Gayle began the trek across the pavement to the covered sidewalk, where the men were still working to a light refrain of bland, pop-country music. She got closer and snuck an actual look at them.

The one with the drill was wearing safety glasses and focused upward on his task. His light gray T-shirt was lifted thanks to his overhead efforts and her eyes went straight to the perfect strip of exposed skin. He was tan and fit. The lower part of his abs she was ogling flexed as he continued drilling or whatever it was he was doing.

Gayle let her gaze slide upward, slowing her walk. The man's face was covered in a light beard, barely more than stubble. His jaw was square and set to his task. His shoulders were broad. His neck and face also nicely bronzed. His eyes…

Gayle blinked and took a step back when she realized he'd stopped the drill and had lifted his safety glasses to stare back at her. The ill-timed step sent her left foot down off the sidewalk and her ankle rolling in seconds. The bolt of agony made her gasp. But it was nothing compared to the actuality of finding herself on her ass, half on, half off the sidewalk. The expensive water bottle rolled away from her, coming to a clanging rest under the work platform. The tarmac burned her left hand while her right kept a death grip on the mat and towel.

Pam was at her side and pulling her up within a half-second, but the half-second she sat, sprawled like a turtle on its back and still eye-locked with the man — the young man, she self-corrected — on the platform was one of the longest of her life. Second only to the one she'd experienced on her way home from work, cruising along the Pacific Coast Highway, that had set her on this current, shitty path.

"Jesus," she muttered, staring down at her swelling ankle.

The men had stopped work. The one with the drill climbed down and retrieved her errant water bottle, handing it to her with a wide, perfect smile. Pam jostled her arm to remind her to lift it and take the thing from him. The other guy leaned over the platform railing, grinning at the small crowd of women that had gathered, all holding the same version of Gayle's bundle of supplies. She lifted her arm, trying not to meet the man's eyes. But she did. And they were, indeed, the exact shade of light coppery-brown she'd seen before she'd done the super-klutz move.

"Ma'am," he said, giving his yellow construction worker's hat a little dip. "You all right?"

His voice was like the purest honey—smooth, rich and somehow soothing. She swayed when she leaned her weight on her injured ankle, but it wasn't because of her foot. "Ma'am?" The man put a hand on her arm, but Pam and the others hustled her inside when the studio owner appeared at the door, concern in her eyes.

"Gayle, here, sit down." The woman's soft voice worked its way past the unwelcome and unexpected rush of memory that had almost made her pass out on the sidewalk. She did as she was told and took the cool glass of water offered to her. She held it, staring down into it, doing her best, therapy-induced mental tricks to muscle past the voice, the touch, the laugh, all the sensations she'd associated with, and adored about, her husband.

All the things she'd taken for granted.

Finally, she sipped and nodded thanks to the efficient woman who'd shooed all the gawkers away to give her space to breathe. She drank the entire glass, then leaned back, pressing her head against the front window. "Thanks, Helen," she said when the studio owner placed a small bag of ice on her aching ankle. "I don't know if I can..."

A sharp rap behind her made her yelp and flinch. Helen smiled and calmly replaced the ice bag where it had been. "Your fan club wants to know if you're okay," she said, giving someone behind Gayle a small wave.

"My...what?" Gayle turned and saw the beautiful young man's eyes, staring at her with concern. He lifted his thumb and treated her to his wide, gorgeous smile. Then turned it down and made a fake sad face, pointing to her. She sucked in a breath, allowing herself another second to appreciate his physical perfection—shoulders even broader than she'd thought tapering to a slim waist, long legs covered in workman's denim, steel-toed boots. The works. He made an exaggerated shrug which tugged a smile to her lips in spite of her intention not to encourage him.

God, he's probably all of twenty years old. Stop staring, you sick cougar.

From his place up on the platform, the other worker gazed down on all the incoming yogis with eagerness. Gayle sighed and did a halfway thumbs-up and pointed to the ice on her ankle.

"*Sorry,*" the man's lips said without sound. Gayle found herself fixated on their extreme fullness. When she realized she was staring and fantasizing about what they might feel like, her entire body flushed hot. She turned away from him, mortified at herself, pressed both hands to her face, squeezed her eyes shut and focused on greeting all the incoming students instead of the much-too-handsome-for-his-own-good young man behind her.

Chapter Two

"I'm gonna give it a try," Gayle said after ten minutes of ice therapy. "I mean, I can't just sit here." She refused to succumb to the extreme temptation to turn around and ogle the man, who, she presumed from the sound, had picked up the drill again.

Helen came around from behind the desk and studied her foot for a few seconds. "Tell you what, see how you get on during the warm-up, but if it feels weak during the balancing series, just sit those out." Her gaze flickered to the men behind Gayle. "I should tell them to take a break. They can see right into the studio."

Gayle noted most of the women had set up their mats far from the wall separating the lobby from the hot room. The fact that anyone walking by could always peer into the room and see the sweaty, sometimes half-naked humans suffering through their practice was never far from Gayle's consciousness. But today, it seemed even more alarming.

"Yeah, but I guess they're not working for you, right?"

"No, they're not. The landlord has done so many great things — new parking lot, new roofs, new facades. And now whatever it is they're doing up there."

Gayle had to bite the inside of her cheek not to turn around and see what Helen was smiling at. Because she already knew. And she couldn't allow herself to look at him again. *Ever.*

She rose and put her weight on the less-swollen ankle. It held, so she lifted her right foot to see how much it could take. "Ankles are incredibly flexible joints," Helen said, holding out a hand just in case Gayle toppled over again. "And you've been coming every other day for a solid two years now, Gayle. It's a testament."

"Yeah, it's something," she said. "It's saved me in a lot of ways." She smiled at the slight, dark-haired woman who was beaming at her. "You know that better than anyone."

Helen patted her arm, gave one last glance up at the men who were, if their noises were any indication, busy at their job again, then held open the hot room door so Gayle could make her way inside. The room was packed 'ass to nose', as one of her fellow yogis liked to say. There were a couple of tiny spaces she could take farther into the room. But one giant swath of real estate remained unclaimed, right in front of the glass doors. Without a thought, Gayle plopped her mat onto it, spread out her towel then eased off the light T-shirt she'd been wearing over her sports bra and spandex, letting it drop to the floor.

She sat in the heat and silence for a few minutes, gathering her thoughts and concentrating on the ninety minutes ahead. The drilling sounds were muted, thanks to the half-wall and doors between her and the sound. But they were still out there, their platform and bodies blocking the sunlight that usually streamed through the glass doors into the studio at this hour.

When Helen flipped on the lights and requested everyone stand and prepare for the breathing exercise, Gayle smiled at her friend, who gave her a quick thumbs-up on her way to the front of the room. The heat settled on her skin in its usual fashion, causing a light sheen of sweat to break out on her arms. She rolled her sore ankle, pleased it did seem to have bounced back, even if her embarrassment over it would likely never fade.

At that split second, preparing for the warm-up, letting the familiar dialogue and patter of the instructor soothe her into a semi-happy—or at least a non-thinking—place in her head, she glanced out of the doors. Hard not to, considering she was bumped up against them, the room was so damn full. Having almost, but not quite, forgotten the existence of the too-young, too-hot man who'd made her fall over and almost lose her water bottle like some kind of a lame ingénue, she startled when she discovered he was staring straight at her, his mouth half hanging open.

Heat rushed through her as she did a quick assessment of herself. Realizing she was at least three seconds behind on the breathing exercise, she shifted her gaze to the bank of mirrors across the front of the hot room. She was wearing one of her new bras—*thank God for small favors*. One of those currently trendy, multi-strappy across the back things with a small bit of padding in the front, which helped her slightly flat chest seem less so. Her shorts were the expensive brand, with the goofy pseudo-Greek letter logo thing on the back she could never for the life of her remember the name of. They were a deep, sapphire blue, matching the bra.

She glared at herself a few seconds, then caught up with the rhythm of the warm-up, smiling at Helen when the woman shot her a concerned glance between instructions. But instead of her usual calm, focused self, she felt more rattled than a kid on the first day of school. Her breathing was off, strained. She was wobbly on her feet. It took her straight back to her earliest days in here, when she'd been so blind with grief it was all she could to do get up every morning and provide her physical self with basic nutrition.

Tears threatened.

Fuck this guy. I refuse to let him get into my head like this.

She tried to catch Helen's eye, to let her know she was all right but had to get some cool air into her lungs. But in the end, she just leaned on the door and pushed her way out into the lobby. Her skin pebbled in the air conditioning, making her shiver. The tears came and she let them. She'd learned that much about herself. Holding them back made it worse. She'd had more crying jags in this particular lobby than in the chic leather chair at her therapist's office.

She looked up after a few seconds, grateful it had been a mild bout, understanding how they came and went with brutal regularity — even now, almost three later. When she leveled her gaze at the young — too young — man still outside the window, she noted he had his hard hat and safety glasses off and was staring straight at her.

His buddy was leaning on the platform railing, ogling the much younger and tighter lady flesh behind her in the hot room, as he should be. Gayle gathered herself, put her hands on her hips and gave the young man a stern look. He blinked in the face of it, ran a hand across his thick crop of dark blond hair and grinned — grinned! — at her.

"*Sorry*," he mouthed, before plunking the hat back on his head and giving his buddy a hard elbow in the side. The other kid frowned, mouthed a few curses then looked at Gayle. He didn't just look. He gave her a rude, blatant, up-and-down stare. She stood still, her hands on her hips, willing the mortification away. She looked hot as shit and she knew it.

Grieving for almost three solid years meant not eating for the better part of eight months, then therapy which included an aggressive exercise program. She'd made other changes too — just for the sake of them, really. She'd stopped eating meat and barely ate any dairy at all. Between her diet, spinning, hot yoga and pilates, her almost-forty self could pass, and had passed, for someone ten years younger.

But the man — *the boy, Gayle. The boy* — and his grin and those eyes and his utter physical perfection had struck her like a thunderbolt. Horrifying, and yet oddly exhilarating at the same time — something she'd not felt since the moment she'd nearly rear-ended someone on the Pacific Coast Highway, listening to the phone call that had changed her entire life.

Her face flushed when she realized the hot guy's buddy was giving her two thumbs-up and a cheesy grin. The other man, the one who'd sent her into such an immature tailspin, was frowning now, first at his co-worker then at her. He stuck his safety glasses on, said something to the other guy then picked up his drill.

Gayle watched them—okay, she ogled them, and wasn't *that* a strange thing to admit—a few seconds longer before ducking back into the hot room with an 'I'm okay' nod to Helen. If she were not mistaken, her scalp was tingly. Her body was still broken out in goosebumps even in the heat. She caught up with the tail end of the breathing warm-up and spent the next eighty-two minutes focused straight ahead, on herself in the mirror as she was supposed to be, even while half her brain was fully aware of the men still working away outside the window.

Chapter Three

"Gayle Connolly, I still can't believe you're here, in my office, asking me to hire you."

She smiled at the silver fox of a man leaning against his massive desk and grinning down at her. "Well, Ben, I guess I decided never working again wasn't the life for me."

"But...okay, never mind. I don't want to ask, lest you talk yourself out of it. When can you start?"

"Well, um...don't you want to, I don't know, ask me some questions? See if I'm a good fit? That I know what I'm doing?"

He laughed—a deep, melodious thing which added to his handsome factor. Gayle shook her head at herself. Ever since the yoga man incident earlier in the day, she'd been thinking the oddest things about the various men she'd encountered. It was as if that weird moment had popped the lid off her formerly healthy, overactive, libido—something she'd assumed was as dead and buried as her husband.

"Don't insult me, Gayle." He went around to his seat and pulled out a file folder, flipping through papers she assumed included her headhunter-provided resume. He stared down at something, shook his head, a distressing, yet familiar sadness filling his eyes before he shut the file.

Gayle set her jaw. She would not allow today's forward motion to get derailed by a bunch of sympathy. She'd had all the fucking sympathy she could stomach in her life—in four or five consecutive lifetimes. She forced herself to smile and wait for him to collect himself. "Well? No questions for me?"

He flinched as if he'd forgotten she was in the room, then sighed. "Okay, how about this one. We have the biggest portfolio of Michigan-based craft beers in the state and we are bloody well drowning in the stuff. Every day another one shows up at my door with their eager faces and samples, hoping just by signing a distribution contract, their futures are made." He leaned back in his seat and steepled his fingertips. "How are we going to separate the wheat from the chaff in all this and stop wasting our sales hours trying to sling useless liquid that won't be the same batch-to-batch and might not even be around in six months?"

She tilted her head. This was exactly what she needed—this challenge. "Well, Ben, as you know, Connelly & Company had the same issue on the West Coast. We had it well before you did. It's not easy, but it will require a hard look at the numbers—I assume you have some decent analysts in here somewhere— plus a few come-to-Jesus meetings with some of the non-sellers. I'm willing to bet you have a nice fat thirty percent cushion of garbage we can slice out with little effort. The next thirty is a little harder to target and get rid of—salesmen get wedded to them sometimes, so you have to listen to their pitches. When you're down to a hard core of real accounts, then we re-focus the sales staff on them."

"Sounds ugly," he said, a frown creasing his forehead.

"It is. But you said it yourself. Your sales people are wheel-spinning, trying to accommodate a ton of breweries that are, in a word, shitty."

"Yes. Agreed." Ben heaved a huge sigh. "I'm really sorry, Gayle. About Ethan and…"

She held up a hand. "I know you are. You've said it before. You and Janet were among the first to arrive for the…funeral stuff and among the last to leave. Don't think I've forgotten it."

"I just never thought you'd get back into it. Since you sold Connolly and decided to come back to Michigan."

"This is my home, Ben. You know that. Ethan was the West-Coaster, not me." She bit her lip. "Listen, I want to help you out. I mean, this is what I did for my own company."

"And you were damn good at it, too."

A flush crept up her neck to her face. She *had* been good at it. She'd started as a merchandiser—the lowest on the totem pole of the sales force—at Connolly and Company, having been lured west by thoughts of sunny days, nights and weekends plus a break from her nosy mother. She'd spent hours building relationships in groceries, gas 'n sips, liquor-lotto stores, various restaurants, just proving she knew what she was doing. She'd reset and tidied beer shelves until a sales position had opened up and she had leapt at it. Five years later, she'd been the top craft beer seller in the company, which was saying something, since Connolly had all the big names in the Bay Area market. Two years later, she'd been named brand manager for three of the biggest breweries, and a short year later she'd made sales manager for the entire craft beer portfolio.

She'd loved her life—her, a small town, mid-Western girl making a real living on the West Coast in an industry she adored. She'd had a cute, miniscule apartment overlooking the Golden Gate Bridge, as much money as she'd ever seen in one place, her own friends, a cute little car, the works. She'd been the opposite of the girl she'd read about in the romance novels who gets swept off her feet by the company CEO or whatever the hell. She would buy her own jewelry, cars and vacations.

But it hadn't lasted. Nope, it sure hadn't.

Gayle blinked fast, fending off tears, while Ben poured her a glass of water and handed it to her, along with a tissue, without a word. She took it and sipped, then set it on the glass table to her left. "I need this, Ben."

"Well, I think the feeling is mutual." He held out a hand. "Welcome to TriCities Distribution. I'll repeat my original question—when can you start?"

She stared at his hand a second, giving herself the time to consider it all. She'd gotten used to not working—to doing whatever the hell she pleased any time of the day. Having more money than God helped. When she gripped his palm, something inside her shifted ever so slightly, allowing a sliver of light to shine into the darkness she'd been inhabiting for two years, ten months, six days and…she checked the Patek Philippe heirloom watch Ethan's mother had given her for a wedding present…two and a half hours.

"I can start Monday," she said, surprising herself with the strength of her voice.

"Good," he said. "Great." He let go of her hand and his face rearranged itself into sympathetic lines again. She frowned at him. "Sorry. Don't worry. This is not a mercy job. Unless you consider working for me a bit of a mercy." He held out his suit-clad arms, taking in his expensively outfitted office.

"Hardly," she said, rising to her feet. "False modesty is annoying, Ben."

"Yes, ma'am." He grinned. "Hey, how about dinner this weekend? I know Janet would love to have you over."

"Maybe," she said. "I need to…take care of a few things before I start. Including a trip out to…out west. To sort of wrap a few things up."

"Right. Okay. Got it." His face reddened.

She smiled, marveling at how her widowed status could reduce grown human beings to stuttering middle schoolers. She hesitated a few seconds while he shuffled papers and calmed down.

"Gayle, I can't tell you how much we needed someone just like you here. I mean, I would have asked a year ago if I even thought you'd…" He paused, smiled and resumed his alpha male mantle. "Anyway, why don't you stop down at HR before you leave and get all the paperwork crap going so you don't have to mess with it Monday?"

"I will, thanks." She shouldered her bag and was headed for his door when he stopped her.

"Oh, shit, I mean…we didn't even talk salary."

She turned back to him, one eyebrow raised. She knew they hadn't, but it was a minor detail to her at this point. "What does the job pay, Ben?"

"A hundred-ten base, plus quarterly bonuses based on performance, which I am certain will be no problem for you."

"Okay, I'll take it."

"Wow, that was easy." He had his hands stuck in his trouser pockets, his face quizzical. "I would have paid more."

"I know you would have," she said with a smile. "I'll hit the HR paperwork and see you on Monday morning."

"Yeah, great. Okay. Super."

"Relax, Ben. What I have isn't catching." She winced. "I'm sorry."

"Understandable. I just don't know how…"

"You'll get used to it." Irrational anger was filling her head, making her ears hot and her skin clammy. "I'll go now. And thanks, Ben. I think we'll work well together." She had to get out of there before she screamed. *Maybe this isn't such a great idea after all.*

No. It was. It was the only idea. She had to do something with herself. And this was what she knew. No matter how utterly awful it was going to be rebuilding herself in this business—Ethan's business. Their business.

She leaned against the wall, holding the tissue to her lips, wondering where the nearest bathroom was. The spasm—which was what it was, a spasm of grief that clutched at her viscera and left her gasping and spent—faded fast. It happened more often now—the fast fading. Which made her feel guilty and pissed off.

It was one of the reasons she'd decided to take the ashes out to the mountains herself. She couldn't just leave the damn things in their fancy box on her mantel in Michigan. Ethan had been a California boy through and through. And she needed to put him back there, where he belonged. She had the private plane booked and on standby, waiting for the right moment. And now the moment had come, about twenty minutes ago, when she'd agreed to go back to work in the beer business, as sales director for the biggest distributor in Michigan.

Later, she sat in her silk PJs and sipped a glass of Pappy Van Winkle, with her other hand resting on the box in her lap. The box that contained the ashes of what was left of her life.

Chapter Four

One month later

"Hey, Gayle, would you look at this for me?"

Gayle glanced up from her computer screen, irritated by the interruption coming during her mandated two hours of quiet in the late afternoon. An especially important time in which she was on the verge of making the second level of cuts out of their beer book. The first wave had been easy. TriCities had gotten greedy. Taken on way more products than they could fairly represent and sales were down across the board. So, she'd cut and slashed without mercy.

But it had to be done, and most of the sales staff were grateful for it.

This next round would prove more difficult. Some of these brands had real fans amongst the retailers. She'd made her list, run it by Ben and was going to present it during the next day's sales meeting, but with the caveat that every sales person had her ear if they wanted to make a case for one brand or another. What they didn't know was if they came at her with a lot of 'oh my God we can't cut these guys they're awesome', she would ask one question.

'Okay, are they awesome enough for you to tie your next quarterly bonus to it? No? Okay, not so awesome then. Yes? Great. You're now their brand manager. Bring me a turn-around plan in forty-eight hours, complete with a budget.'

If they actually took these steps, most times the sales would go up and she'd agree to keep the account. If not, they were yesterday's news. The current craft beer market was drowning the public in options. It was time to contract and focus on the breweries who knew what the hell they were doing.

"Sure," she said, holding out her hand for the proffered computer tablet. She studied the quarter's reports, signed her name to them for the various taxation authorities then handed the thing back with as genuine a smile as she could manage. "Would you mind?" She pointed to the propped-open glass door. "I need some time."

The woman nodded and backed out, closing the door behind her. Gayle rolled her head around, trying to work out some of the kinks in her neck. Her eyes burned from staring at the screen for so long, so she got up and paced around the office, wishing she didn't have to work in a fishbowl, but realizing Ben prided himself on his super modern building with its half-opaque glass walls separating the upper management from the plebe lands.

As she stared out of the window onto the bustling warehouse below, her phone buzzed with a text. Figuring it for one of her prima donna brewery accounts, she ignored it, but when it happened again, then a third time, she grabbed the thing with a curse. Noting who it was, she smiled, hit Call and stuck her wireless earbuds into her ears. "Hey, friend. What's up?"

"Hey yourself," Evelyn Fitzgerald said. "How goes it with the poison pen over there?"

She winced and sat in her ergonomically correct, ugly desk chair. "Word's out, eh?"

"And how. They're calling you the Evil Queen, among other things."

"I can only imagine."

"It's the right thing. We get it. But we're at the top of that food chain...at least I hope we are."

"Of course you are. Since you've taken over sales and marketing, you're printing money."

"Helps to have good brewers..."

"Oh, hell, those guys are a dime a dozen now."

Evelyn chuckled. "Don't let Hoffman hear you say that."

"Don't worry, I won't. I thought he left anyway. Opening the restaurant with Elle in Detroit."

"He still consults. He's out here two or three times a month. He's too much of an anal control freak to give us up completely."

"I'm sure." She sipped from her water bottle. "What's up, then? Not a problem with our sales people, I assume." There wasn't. Gayle knew where the company's bread was buttered, and Fitzgerald Brewing Company held one of the biggest knives for that job. She rode herd big time on the large account brand managers—probably too much, but Ben had said she should run things like she saw fit. She was the boss. So she acted like it. As a result, of course, she had no real friends here. Only people who admired her with the same level of energy that they hated and were terrified of her.

She heaved a too-loud sigh.

"Whew, sounds serious," Evelyn said. "Anyway, so, I'm calling to invite you out."

"Out?" Gayle finished the water and put her high-heel-clad feet up on the glass desk top. "Who goes 'out' anymore? Don't you have a kid?"

"Yes. And a nanny. And a husband who's headed to Denver for the week. So I'm bored."

"Okay. What is there to do around here, anyway?" She grinned, enjoying the banter. If anyone knew what there was to do around here, Gayle did. It was her job, after all.

"I say we go dancing."

"Dancing? Are you insane?"

"Only moderately. What do you say? I think I'll be fun!"

"Hmmm...." Gayle pondered this. She used to love nothing more than going out to drink, dance, party, play poker—everything. She'd done it with girlfriends. She'd done it, and more, with Ethan. But she hadn't gone out for fun since... "Yes. Let's do it." She put her feet on the floor. "Where?"

"Nexus," Evelyn said, naming one of the chic dance clubs in reviving downtown Grand Rapids.

Gayle whistled. "You don't fuck around, do you?"

"Nope. I'm going to get a ride there. We can share a ride home. They open at ten. But we need to dress for it, you know...kinda sexy and shit."

"Good God. I don't know."

"You do, too. You look like a million bucks, Gayle, and you know it. I've finally lost my baby weight. Let's go shake our asses and flirt with some boys, whaddaya say?"

"You are married to the most awesome man in the immediate universe and you want to…"

"Yes, I am. But if you think he's not flirting his ever-loving hot ass off in Denver, you're delusional. It's not like I'm looking for a hook-up. I just want to dance and drink and not worry about anything for a few hours."

"And you figured I could use that kind of thing too, I suppose." The familiar anger was rolling around in her head, but she forced it away.

"Well, yeah, kinda."

Gayle sighed. "You're probably right."

"I know I am. Do you have something to wear?"

"I do have other things besides widow's weeds, you know." She winced at her tone but knew Evelyn wouldn't care.

"Good. Make it sexy and hydrate during the day. I'll see you there Friday night. Ten-thirty."

"There won't be a rope line, will there?"

"Of course there will be. And between us, we'll be jumping that son-of-a-bitch."

In spite of her misgivings, aggravation and mild panic about going out in a sexy dress for dancing after so long, she laughed. "I love you, Evelyn."

"Of course you do. See you Friday."

Gayle put her phone down on her desk slowly, her ears ringing and her face hot with the possibility of a fun night out. She caught sight of her face in the sleeping laptop computer screen. "Jesus," she muttered, leaning closer and getting a better look at herself. She frowned, picked up her phone and made two quick appointments for a deep facial and a hair color touch-up. *I can't go out looking like a sad widow, now can I?*

When the thought hit her brain, she blinked at herself and put her hand over her lips. "Oh shit, Ethan, you fucking asshole." Tears flowed, burning her cheeks. She let them. It was the best way, really.

Chapter Five

Friday arrived way too fast for Gayle's nerves. Even after she'd added a massage to the facial the evening before, even after ninety minutes in the hot yoga room and a day spent on the road visiting some of her more robust retailers — once one of her favorite things about her job — she was a frazzled, jumpy mess. She couldn't choke down her lunch but made sure to drink plenty of water during the day. She was no rookie when it came to imbibing booze and anticipated tonight would mean martinis — real ones, like, with gin — which meant her body needed to be prepared for the onslaught.

At three-thirty, she shut her laptop and sat for a few minutes, using her therapy-taught meditation methods to gather herself. It was ridiculous, all this worry. What in the hell did she have to lose, anyway? She was going out with a friend for a few drinks and some tipsy dancing with strangers. No biggie.

A chill shot down her spine. She placed her hands on the glass desktop beside her computer, staring at her recently painted fingernails — red, her signature color for such things — and made a serious attempt not to freak all the way out. She had no business doing any of this. She was a thirty-six-year-old widow, well past her prime.

No, this wasn't about impressing anyone. This was about having fun. And she deserved to have some fun. Evelyn was right about that, as she usually was. Gayle smiled at the thought of her friend, who'd begun her career in this very company not too long ago, now married to and working alongside the owner of one of the most successful breweries in Michigan — hell, in the entire Midwest these days — with a beautiful little baby girl. Evelyn and Austin had been steadfast friends during the early, woozy days around the funeral and after. She was lucky to have them.

She was lucky.

Right.

Gayle curled her fingers into her palms and pressed both fists into the cold glass.

Stop it. Stop it now, Gayle Jackson Connolly. You have more money than some entire cities. You can go anywhere, do anything you want. If you wanted to quit this job today, you could walk away and not give it a half a second's thought. There are people within half a mile of you right now who are hungry, desperate to pay rent, utilities, medical bills. Focus on helping them, not on how hard it is to breathe every time you remember your husband is dead.

She did help, of course. She donated the value of her entire salary every month to several charities that focused their efforts on homeless families, abused women and hungry kids. She was even on the board of a couple of those charities and had begun to dutifully attend boring meetings in the name of paying some of the wealth of her life back to the universe, somehow.

And all this on top of the Connolly Foundation she'd set up, thinking she'd turn herself into a Melinda Gates-style widow, traveling around, writing, talking, throwing money at starving children.

All of it was intended to help others, but also herself — to provide a suitable distraction for the God-awful reality of her loneliness, the mountain of her grief, the canyon of her despair. It had, to some extent, but of course, now here she was doing the eight-to-six workday drudge again, even though she didn't have to.

She sighed and rose slowly, feeling her knees and hips release the tension she'd balled herself into in the last few minutes. A quick glance at her tablet revealed the date. Her well-trained mind rolled through the ongoing countdown she'd been living with since the accident. She was coming up on three years. *Great.*

She picked up her tablet, stuffed it into her bag and headed for the closed door.

"Have a nice weekend, Gayle," her admin said with a wide smile.

Gayle blinked at her, suddenly unable to remember the woman's name. Then it hit her. "Thanks, Susan. You too." She shook her head at herself all the way to the flight of metal stairs down to the main lobby. She'd fired the first two admins. They'd been too slow to keep up with her. *No wonder these people are terrified of me. Evil Queen indeed.*

She smiled vaguely at all the people wishing her a nice weekend on her way to the building's entrance, accepting she hardly knew any of them. At least outside their typical contexts — in sales meetings or in one-on-one rah-rah get-your-ass-in-gear coaching sessions. She shouldered her way out of the air-conditioned interior into the oppressive heat of a late-July afternoon, her mind scrolling through the various excuses she'd give Evelyn. There was no way in this universe or the next two she'd be going out tonight. It was just too ridiculous to consider.

She made it all the way home, only half aware that part of her had been looking forward to tonight's little adventure.

"Home," she called out, putting her bag down and her keys and watch in the bowl on the landing space in her mother's kitchen. She leafed through the stack of mail, then poured herself a huge glass of water, furious that her pulse kept racing and her heartbeat pounded in her ears.

"Hey, honey." Her mother, a well-preserved seventy-year-old, paused to kiss her cheek briefly in her act of flipping on the kettle for more tea.

"How's the new book coming?" Gayle leaned against the sink and studied the woman who stood staring out of the window, in her writing zone, as Gayle well knew by now.

"What? Oh, pretty well, I think. How was your day?"

"Fine, thanks." They stood in comfortable silence until the kettle sang out. Her mother poured the water over a fresh chamomile tea bag, smiled in Gayle's general direction and wandered back toward her office.

Realizing any sort of distracting conversation with her mother would be futile right now, Gayle glanced at the hot yoga schedule she'd stuck on the cluttered fridge front and decided this would be a double day. She'd gone to the six a.m., but she needed something more to calm her, to get her to the hour she had to get primped and pretty and go out with her friend. She ran up the stairs to the room she'd re-inhabited in the last three years, changed into another of her wildly expensive sports bras and shorts outfits, pulled a sundress over them and headed back downstairs.

As focused as she was on her goal—getting out of the door and across town for the four-thirty practice time—she nearly plowed right over the woman standing at the foot of the stairs, hands on her hips, her faded blue eyes narrowed. "Jesus, Mom, what the hell?" Gayle stepped to the side, her mind already calculating she'd be lucky to make it in time, if she were already in the car and pointed toward the studio.

"I've made a decision about something," Trudie Jackson declared.

"Oh? Can it wait a bit? I want to get to—"

Her mother held up a long-fingered hand. Gayle swallowed a sigh. Living here for the last few years had been a life-saving move, but there were plenty of times her knee-jerk, adolescent responses to her mother burst out of her.

"This is important, Gayle. Sit."

"I thought you were writing." She heard the whine in her voice, but it was too late to do anything about it now.

"I am, but it can wait." Gayle's mother was a millionaire in her own right, a multiple *New York Times* best-selling author of feel-good, sexy romances for the last twenty-plus years. She wrote under two different pseudonyms, boasted an army of loyal, rabid fans and had been featured repeatedly on national TV as the world's oldest living erotic romance author. Her latest claim to fame was that one of her books would be turned into a premiere cable series within the next two years.

She was a five-foot-nothing whirlwind of energy, bustle and charm and while a single mother working two waitressing jobs, had raised Gayle, making sure her girl had the best clothes, healthiest food and all the normal, teenaged fun her money could buy. When she'd finally found an agent while Gayle had been busy drinking her way through college, she'd burst onto the romance scene and never looked back. Gayle was proud of her, but found it ironically hilarious that Trudie was the most cynical woman about men and love she'd ever encountered.

"Okay." She sat, tapping her fingertips on the kitchen table. Trudie stared at them. Gayle stopped tapping and put her hands in her lap, biting back the sharp rebuke.

"You need to move out," her mother said, with a typical bluntness but using words that shocked Gayle to her core. She must have looked as startled as she felt, because her mother reached over and grabbed her hands, clenching them tight inside her own. "Honey, I love you but this..." She let go and waved her arms around, indicating the cute but slightly cramped Cape Cod-style home Gayle had grown up in, left and come back to heal. "This isn't good for you anymore. You need to get out, learn to live on your own again. Find...find some fun."

"Mom," Gayle said, her voice breaking in spite of her efforts to remain calm. "What are you... I'm not going to date, if that's what you're talking about."

"Partly, yes, but mostly I mean you need to rejoin the land of the living. It's time, honey."

Tears poured out of Gayle's eyes with no warning. "I think I can decide when that time comes, Mom." She sniffled and swiped at her cheeks.

"No, I don't think you can." Trudie sat back and crossed her arms.

"Jesus, why don't you tell me how you really feel?"

"I am," her mother replied. "And I'm sorry to have to be this person, but you're working again, which is great, so it's time you moved out, got your own place and got on with your life."

"Okay. Your opinion is noted." Gayle rose, unable to say anything else. "I'm going to yoga."

"Gayle, honey, wait."

She hesitated at the door out to the garage and squeezed her eyes shut, mentally yelling and cursing at Ethan for something like the zillionth time for getting on that fucking private jet in the first place. Her mother's hand rested on her shoulder, a gesture which sent her spiraling back almost three years to when she'd spend hours staring into the air around her, willing the whole thing to be nothing but a vivid nightmare. Trudie would sit with her in silence as long as Gayle needed, seeming to sense her desire for a bit of peace amidst all the babble – the arrangements, the double whammy of memorial services in Cali and Michigan, the never-ending parade of sympathetic faces, the tears. Sometimes she'd simply touch Gayle on the shoulder, just like she was doing now, as if to anchor her to the earth.

"I get it, Mom. But I…I need to get to my yoga class." She shrugged Trudie's hand off her and barely made it in time for the breathing exercise and Helen's raised eyebrow at her double practice for the day.

As she lay in her final savasana, sweat pouring off her, her entire body a giant, grateful wet noodle and her mind blissfully blank, she realized her mother was right. As usual. She should move out and get on with her life again. She rolled to her side and closed her eyes at the realization she was, indeed, moving on, but without the man who'd spent the better part of two years convincing her to love him back, only to lose him seven years into their marriage. And to what? To convenience. It was more 'convenient' for him to travel by private jet from California to Florida so he could meet with the latest distributorship he was buying. It was more 'convenient' to combine it with a trip to Disney.

She heard a strange noise and realized it was coming from her, so she clapped her hand over her mouth and attempted to shove the inevitable, encroaching memory dump out of her head. At least the part of it she could cope with thinking about. Sadly, there was still some of the day's horror she still refused to acknowledge. Sometimes she believed she never would.

"Gayle?" Helen's soft voice and cool hand on her shoulder made her flinch, then roll onto her stomach so she could get up from the soaking wet towel. "You all right?"

"No," she said in a tight whisper. "But that's not your fault." She grabbed her mat, towel and drained water bottle and stumbled through the now-empty room out into the cool back hallway, avoiding the sympathy stares of everyone around her. Jesus, would there ever come a day she could get through and not turn into a sodden, weepy mess? Even she was getting sick of herself. And her mother was too, since she was prepared to kick Gayle out on the streets.

She rolled her eyes at her inner hyperbole. She could buy any piece of property in this town she wanted. Resolved, but with the sort of knee-jerk reaction she knew she might regret down the road, she pulled out her phone and found a familiar name. After tugging her sundress down over her damp skin, she grabbed her stuff and put the phone to her ear. "Yo, Hettinger, you busy?"

"Never for a pretty lady," the man's deep voice replied. "What can I do for you?"

"I want to buy something downtown…a loft or something. I know you live down there so…"

"Well, we're about to move once the house renovation from hell gets done. But not too far away. And Kayla's taking over the loft."

"Is there anything else for sale right now?"

"I'll find something for you. What do you want to spend?"

"I…don't care. But I need something fast. One bedroom is fine, two is preferred. A view of something other than the top of a building would be ideal."

"I think I know just the place. A few buildings down from mine. One of my buddies owns a couple and his tenants are about to leave."

"I don't want to rent it."

"I know. I'll tell him. He'll sell…when I tell him to."

"You have that kind of power, now, eh, big stuff?"

"Yeah, I guess I kind of do. Listen, Gayle, I heard you were working again, for TriCities. I think that's great."

"Yes, I am and thanks." She sat in the hot car and gnawed at her lower lip.

"So this place I'm thinking of will probably run you at least eight hundred…"

"Thousand?" She gulped, still unable to grasp the breadth and depth of her new-found, wholly unwanted wealth.

"Yeah. That okay?"

She sucked in a long breath, blew it out and reminded herself she could probably buy the whole building he was talking about and still have plenty of money to live on for the rest of her natural life. Ethan had been wealthy when she'd met him and had run the San Francisco-based distributorship himself mainly because it was a business he truly enjoyed, not because he needed a salary. His grandfather had been one of the original real estate barons of the West Coast and his father had grown the business so well, Ethan had been born with a dozen silver spoons. But he'd been made to work for his father from the time he was sixteen – he'd done maintenance on buildings, endless hours of yardwork, then graduated to the accounting side, and rental management while he was in college.

When Grant Connolly had jumped into the beer and wine distribution business with a partner, his son Ethan had found his calling. He'd taken over, after working his way up through the ranks in a way not dissimilar to Gayle's – merchandising, sales, brand management. When she'd started working for his company, he'd been CEO for over fifteen years and remained a perpetual member of 'California's 'most desired bachelors' club. Until he had laid eyes on her, of course.

After their Hawaii wedding, he'd set up a trust in her name, plus one other, over the course of their life together, and had declared her his sole heir in the unlikely event of his early death. It had shocked his parents, but they'd loved their son, and her, eventually, so they'd not contested anything.

She was worth something in the neighborhood of forty-eight million bucks. A mind-numbing sum of money managed by a slew of smart people she met with quarterly to review how they were growing her fortune, while she played a direct role in the management of the charitable foundation. A different set of people were in charge of her daily monetary requirements, including paying credit card bills she never saw.

Her married life to Ethan had been cushy in the extreme. They'd worked side-by-side at the distribution company, but he was prone to whisking her off to France or the Bahamas on a moment's notice — although he always made sure to coordinate it with her assistant and her travel schedule. They'd had a beautiful home overlooking the ocean, two cars — each — plus someone to clean and even cook for them if they wanted it. Her walk-in closet next to her beautiful bathroom had been a work of art, kept filled with all manner of clothing, shoes and bags. And Ethan had loved nothing more than buying her jewelry. She'd gotten rid of most of it, only hanging on to pieces that didn't hurt her soul when she looked at them.

But while all of it had seemed wonderful, beyond anyone's wildest fantasy of a fairy tale, she'd rejected it at first. She hadn't believed the man had wanted her for anything more than sex — something they'd had a lot, and early on in their relationship. At times, lying wide awake late at night and missing him so much she could barely think straight, she would remind herself of the fact *she* had cost them at least three years of marital happiness with her foolish stubbornness.

It hit her again now, hard, and right between her eyes, making her sway in her seat. "Yes, Trent. It's fine. Let me know when I can see it."

"You got it, gorgeous." Silence descended between them while Gayle tried not to burst into tears — again.

"Anything else I can do? Hey, do you want to come up to the lake house sometime? We're going up—"

"Nothing more for now, thanks," she interrupted him, unwilling to listen to a half-hearted invite for a weekend away. She knew from Evelyn that Trent had a new wife, Melody, who was pregnant, and Taylor, his teenaged daughter from his first marriage, was giving them fits over her college choices, or lack of them. The last thing they needed was to feel obligated to entertain her. "Tell Melody and Taylor I said hi."

"Will do. I'll text you once I get something set up for you to see."

"Thanks, Trent. Talk to you soon. Bye." She hung up before he could say anything else, took a few seconds to grip her steering wheel, then pushed the ignition button and listened to the expensive German-engineered engine purr to life. She'd killed a couple of hours with the extra yoga practice. Now she had to figure out how to kill three more before she could start getting ready for the big night out.

Chapter Six

"Come on in," Gayle said when her mother knocked on her bedroom door at nine-thirty. She was standing in front of the full-length mirror she'd had her whole life, marveling at the stranger who seemed to be peering back at her from its reflective depths. She didn't turn to face Trudie, just kept smoothing her hands over her seemingly non-existent hips in the silly, expensive designer dress she'd bought the night before, after her facial and massage.

It was made of a smooth, silvery material with miniscule beading that reflected the light and left her shoulders, upper chest and a long expanse of her leg exposed in a way she hadn't really taken into account when she'd swooped into the downtown boutique and said she needed something 'for a night out dancing'.

The sales woman had taken a long, head-to-toe look at her and pulled a single dress from a rack. When she'd held it out so Gayle could try it on, she'd been so damn relieved this was going to be a relatively painless process, she'd barely looked at herself in the dressing room mirror. The sales woman had sucked in a breath when Gayle had pulled back the heavy velvet curtain to get an opinion. "What?"' she'd asked, tugging at the clingy fabric. "Is it awful?"

"No. Quite the opposite." She'd encouraged Gayle to step out into the room. "You look incredible in it. You must work out."

"Yes, well..." Gayle had tugged at her scraggly ponytail and noted in the gigantic mirror that her face looked exactly like it had been loofahed by a coral reef. "God," she'd said, covering her cheeks with her hands.

"Exactly," the sales woman had said, pulling a shimmery shawl from another rack and draping it across Gayle's bare shoulders. "You're exquisite."

But Gayle had barely taken in the dress, or rather, the lack of it. She'd felt shaky and all kinds of wrong. The rest of the staff and a couple of fellow shoppers had gathered around and made many ooing and ahing noises. She'd purchased it, the shawl and a pair of admittedly beautiful high heels in the same color, with silvery ribbons she would tie around her ankles – all of it a pure, fifteen-minute impulse-slash-guilt buy. She couldn't even recall what the whole shebang had cost her, she'd been so eager to get the hell out of there.

"Wow," her mother said with a whistle. "You are stunning."

"I'm practically naked is what I fucking well am." She flopped onto the bed, tears threatening, arms crossed over the sparkly bodice.

"So?" Trudie took her hand and pulled her back to her feet. "All that exercise really shows."

"Everything shows, Mama," she whined, turning to stare at herself, surprised all over again when the stranger looked back at her. She'd had her brown hair touched up with a few reddish highlights, and cut to reduce the split ends she'd let gather for the years since she'd last darkened the door of a salon. It dropped smooth and straight past her shoulders. She pulled it back, relieved to see she did, indeed, seem to still be in this room, in this slutty dress.

"Calm down," Trudie said, pulling her hand away so her hair fell down her back. "Look at me." She took Gayle's hands in hers and held on tight. Ever the dutiful daughter, Gayle met her gaze. "This is what you need. You have to get out from under the frumpy hair, sterile business suits, boring shoes. You used to be fun, remember?"

"I also used to be married. I also used to be a — "

Trudie frowned but tightened her hold on Gayle's hands. "You know what I mean. Stop fighting me on this. I'm proud of you, honey. So very proud. You've done the worst thing any woman should have to do — you've buried everything you loved about your life. But it's not coming back. It's time…" She gave Gayle's hands one last squeeze and let go. "You're only thirty-six years old. You owe it to yourself to move past this, just a little. I don't mean to forget. You'll never do that." She tucked a thick lock of Gayle's hair behind her left ear and cupped her chin. "I'll never forget them either, so I can't even imagine what you're going through, but I do know you are still alive. And you deserve to enjoy your life again."

Gayle sniffled, thankful the ubiquitous tears seemed to be dormant at the moment. A relief on one level, but alarming on another. With a long exhalation, she turned back to look at herself, running her hands down the shiny material. "I look okay?" She turned left, then right, noting that she was indeed wearing this dress like a damn runway model. "I had no idea I'd lost so much weight."

Trudie grabbed a makeup brush and came at her. "Here, let me."

"Mama, I'm fine." She tried to duck away, perfectly happy with her usual minimal foundation and mascara makeup regimen.

"Don't be ridiculous. This is a dance club, not the damn beer warehouse. Sit. Be quiet. Let me work."

Gayle did, and when her mother allowed her to look at herself again, she gasped. "Jesus, Mama." Her eyes were frosty shadowed, lined with smudgy kohl, framed by black lashes. Her high cheekbones were bronzed perfectly. The rest of her skin had a glowing, natural-looking tone. "Fine." She grabbed a brush, but Trudie snatched it away from her.

"Nope. You're perfect. Stop fiddling. Where are your shoes?"

"There." Gayle pointed to the shoebox on the bed. Trudie pulled them out, making her low, admiring whistle again. Gayle rolled her eyes, but took the shoes and slid her feet into them. They were, without a doubt, perfect with the dress. And she figured wearing sexy high heels would be like riding a bike—Ethan used to love it when she dressed up and wore things like this on their many dates all around the world.

But here she was, back in her stodgy, mid-west Cape Cod-style childhood home, putting on sexy shoes, about to go out and 'live her life', whatever the hell *that* meant. She closed her eyes for a split second, waiting for the hot wave of anger to pass. It did, as it always did, so she put on the other shoe, then rose slowly, alarmed at the height of the things for a few seconds until she got her equilibrium back.

"Oh, Gayle," her mother sighed behind her.

"Do *not* cry, Mama. I've made it almost four whole hours without crying and I am not about to start now."

"I won't, I won't."

She took another long look at herself, noting the way the material shimmered every time she moved even a little. Her arms and legs were slim and toned. What remained of her cleavage still seemed a bit too exposed, but she shrugged, figuring if she were going to do this, she was going to do it right. Saying a tiny mental thanks to Evelyn for suggesting this, along with her usual simultaneous curse and declaration of love to her dead husband, she headed downstairs to meet the ride share car she'd called.

"Don't forget this!" Her mother ran down the steps and held out something.

"I've got my bag, ID and a credit card plus a little cash and lipstick. I think I'm good."

But Trudie just waved the tiny zippered pouch at her with a stern expression on her face.

"Go on. It's just a few extras you might need. I never go out without them."

With a sigh, figuring it was a packet of mints and a comb or something, Gayle grabbed it. A familiar yet odd-sounding crinkle from inside the thing hit her ear, making her frown and unzip it. "Mama. Seriously." She pulled out a short strip of condoms, a tiny toothbrush with a matching miniscule tube of paste and a fresh pair of panties. "You are certifiable."

Trudie just grinned and shrugged.

"Wait. You said *you* never go anywhere without this stuff?"

Her mother's grin widened and her eyes twinkled — and not in a grandmotherly way. "I spend a lot of time on the road at book events, you know. And I am not some kind of a celibate saint."

"Oookay, please stop talking now." Her phone beeped, indicating her ride was waiting. She shoved the bizarre collection of stuff into the pouch and stuck it in her bag. "I'm not going to need condoms, that much I can guarantee." The thought of anyone — any man — touching her, kissing her, holding her who was not her dead husband made her mildly nauseated, until a quick flash of memory of a young man on a platform, wearing a hard hat and the world's sexiest grin on his face, made her shiver and her face flush. "Shit. This is nuts."

"Go on. Have fun. Don't do anything I wouldn't do."

Gayle glared at her slight, still pretty mother for a few seconds then blew her a kiss and headed out of the door into the still hot night. As she sat in the passenger seat, worrying the space on her left ring finger where her platinum band had rested for not long enough, she made a decision. Right before the driver pulled up to the front of the teeming sidewalk in front of the club, she plucked the thin chain from her purse and re-fastened it behind her neck. The weight of Ethan's ring dangled right below the dip between her collarbones, its heavy warmth giving her comfort. Before she got out, she thanked the driver, an older woman who'd been happy not to chat, thank God, and touched her fingertips to the ring, sensing the imagined, residual warmth of his skin.

"There you are...holy shitballs, sister, you look incredible!" Evelyn grabbed her arm and hustled her around the long line of people — most of them at least fifteen years younger than she was. She barely had time to register the hate daggers from the crowd before Evelyn had batted her eyelashes at the door guardian and they were ushered inside ahead of everyone else.

The noise, sights and sounds nearly knocked her back on her butt. Not that she wasn't familiar with them. She was. But it had been years since she'd been in a place like this one. It rose three stories, with full balconies, and dancing girls and guys in weird, clear tube-like things that rose and fell from somewhere so high up she couldn't even see it.

It smelled a lot like Abercrombie and Fitch mixed with pot smoke and was freezing cold where she stood. The main bar was a raised platform in what looked to be the smack middle of the gigantic dance floor, but she was willing to bet there were satellites of it on every balcony. A place like this charged triple for drinks and made weak-ass pours so patrons were better off with a beer, or wine, or…

"Martinis!" Evelyn yelled in her ear. "I know I need one. Come on. I reserved us a table upstairs, so we can people watch for a while."

Gayle nodded, still somewhat awed by the chest-pounding beat and the absolute swarm of beautiful young people all around her. It was, in a word, breathtaking—and yet depressing at the same time.

As she followed her friend around the outside of the dance floor to a set of spiral stairs up, she saw several half-hidden corridors under the steps and farther behind, all with slightly waving light velvet curtains. At one point, someone lifted a side and she saw a couple making out. Her face reddened and her scalp tingled at the sight until Evelyn poked her shoulder and motioned upwards. She nodded and minded her own business until she saw the tiny table with the

RESERVED card and two dirty martinis with a bonus bowl of olives on the side.

"You went all out," she shouted over the noise.

Evelyn nodded, handed her one and motioned to the seats. Gayle sat, clinked glasses with her friend, sipped and trained her gaze downward. There was no use pretending they could have a real conversation amidst the noise, so they drank two martinis each and leaned over the railing, taking in the sights. At one point, a waitress brought them two shot glasses of clear liquid and told them the men across the room had paid for them. Gayle flushed hot when the men — handsome, and very young — waved at her and Evelyn.

"Hell to the yeah." Evelyn knocked hers back and swiped at her lips. Gayle studied her friend, using the assistance of two stiff drinks to give her courage.

"What is wrong with you, anyway?" She sniffed the shot glass and shivered. Tequila. *No way. Not after two gin martinis, anyway.* She placed the glass on the table between them and leaned closer to her friend, grabbing her hand and yanking her down so the woman could hear her. "Hey. You. What's wrong?"

Evelyn's eyes filled with tears, but she shook her head so hard, her casual up-do came loose, sending strands of blonde hair cascading down to her shoulders. "I'm not talking about it."

"The hell you're not!" Gayle knew she was hollering, but the thought that she might *not* be the saddest damn person in the room only added to her buzz. She kept a tight hold on Evelyn's hand as she motioned for a passing waiter. "Water," she demanded, pointing to herself and her companion.

When Evelyn attempted to pull away, Gayle tugged her closer until their faces were almost touching over the small table. "Talk to me, woman."

Her friend sighed and looked down at their joined hands. Gayle let her go with a frown.

"I had another miscarriage," she said.

"Another?" Gayle nodded thanks for the two room-temperature water bottles plunked in front of them. She opened them both and took Evelyn's hand again, so she could put hers in it. "Wait. Drink some of this first."

Evelyn sipped. Gayle tipped the bottom of the bottle up until the other woman took a real drink. She took a long gulp of her own, trying to recall if she knew Evelyn and Austin wanted more kids. Rose, their daughter, was almost four, so she supposed it was time. She put the lid back on both their bottles and leaned forward again, motioning so Evelyn would do the same. "I'm sorry. I didn't know there were…others before. How awful for you."

"Yes, well…." Evelyn fiddled with her wedding ring, her earring, her necklace and kept her gaze averted. "You do know that Rose is… I mean, Ross and I…um…"

Gayle held up a hand. "I get it. It's complicated. But Ross found someone and he's happy as a pig in shit, best I can tell."

A ghost of a smile flitted across her friend's face. "Yes. He has and we're really happy for him." She slumped back, letting her long legs, just as exposed as Gayle's, sprawl out in front of her. Gayle frowned at a couple of guys standing nearby, eyeballing them. "That's kind of the problem, I think. I really want to have Austin's child, you know? I mean, he's never acted any other way but as Rose's father. I don't know. I'm too old for this, anyway. I'm sure it's nature's helpful way of reminding me."

Gayle sipped some more, gathering her thoughts. Talk of babies and children was something she avoided like the plague, but her friend was obviously miserable and she was due some time on this side of the sympathy continuum. "So, how many have you had?"

"Three," Evelyn said, sipping and looking down onto the crowd.

"What?" Gayle leaned closer, not sure she'd heard correctly. "Wait, how old are you anyway?"

"Thirty-five."

"That's not too old. Please." She waved a hand, an unwelcome sensation of anger creeping up her spine. "They were early ones, I assume."

Evelyn glanced over at her, her eyes swimming again. She swiped at them, then attempted to put her hair back up, which drew the gaze of several men. Evelyn was a tall, curvy beauty, with a thick mane of blonde hair, deep blue eyes and full lips. It was no wonder she was getting attention. "This last one..." She stopped and made a face. "I guess it was about four months. Messy. Had to go to the outpatient clinic for a...a..."

"My God," Gayle yelped, grabbing her friend's hand. "Why didn't you call me? I would've gone with you."

Evelyn's face fell. "We didn't tell anyone. Austin was with me. It was fine." She met Gayle's eyes. "And I wasn't about to subject you, of all people, to my disaster."

"I'm not... That's bullshit, okay?" Anger flared again, hot and choking. "I'm not some kind of fragile waif, you know. If anything, I've been there, done it. I can handle it. And I want you to ask for my help, if you need it."

A single tear slid down Evelyn's face. Gayle reached over and wiped it away with an encouraging smile. "I'm sorry. I know how hard this is."

"I know you do." Evelyn looked away from her. "I think that guy over there is staring right at you," she whispered. "Look. To my right."

"No," Gayle said, determined not to look even as she did. The man was indeed staring straight at her, his brow furrowed as if he were trying to place her. She treated him to a light smile, then focused back on her friend. "I had four of them," she said. Evelyn's eyes widened.

"Four? Four miscarriages? Jesus, Gayle. I had no idea."

"No one does, except Ethan, of course, and he isn't telling anyone."

Evelyn frowned at her, but Gayle grinned, shocked and yet pleased she'd managed a tiny joke. She patted Evelyn's arm then leaned over the railing, watching the roil and pulse of bodies below them. She put her chin on her hands, realizing the horror of those years had been entirely forgotten, superseded by the worse one that had come later. But the memory of her frustration at her body's seeming lack of basic female functionality filled her mind now. She pushed against Evelyn's shoulder with her own.

"You'll be fine. Don't stop trying."

Evelyn made a snorting noise and finished off her water. "Austin's barely talking to me right now. He says I'm too obsessed with it. Keeps telling me if I'd just 'relax' everything would be fine. Like he can understand this. We had a huge fight before he left. I probably said some things I shouldn't have. Shit." She sighed and wiped another tear off her face.

"Yeah. They don't get it at all. No matter how great they are in other ways." She shoulder-bumped her friend once more. "And he's pretty great. Don't take it for granted."

Evelyn nodded. "I know. You're right. I should just chill out about it."

"Probably." She motioned for the waitress again. "I'm going to have more water, then I'm going to dance." She didn't really want to, but it seemed silly not to, since they were both dressed for it and it actually looked kind of fun down there in the scrum.

Evelyn sat back again and finished her water. "I'm sorry to be a buzz kill."

A laugh burst out of Gayle, surprising her and drawing the eye of the mystery man again. He lifted a dark eyebrow and leaned back against a wall-height bar. She watched him, surprised at herself, but unable to stop. Their second water bottles arrived, along with two more clear liquor shots. Gayle frowned at the man. He shrugged, sipped from a brown beer bottle and turned away from her.

What the hell, why not?

She handed Evelyn one of the shot glasses and held hers up. "Here's to me *not* being the buzz kill for a change. It's a relief, I assure you."

Evelyn met her grin and her glass and they knocked back the booze. Gayle smiled at the sensation of the ice-cold vodka laced with a bit of lemon.

"That was good," Evelyn said, plunking the glass upside down on the table between them.

"Yeah, it was some expensive vodka. I can tell. Tequila is for college kids."

Evelyn sat up straighter and her eyes were shining, but not with tears this time. "Speaking of kids, I say we show the ones down there how this shit is done, my friend." She rose, pulling the gaze of half a dozen men as if she were a giant, female-shaped magnet.

Gayle smiled and joined her, doing her own dude-eyeball-magnet thing. She linked her arm in Evelyn's and they headed for the spiral stairs. "I haven't been dancing in forever," she confessed to her friend.

Evelyn patted her hand, then lead the way down the steps. "Me neither," she said once Gayle was standing next to her once more. "But I hear it's like riding a bike," she said, towing Gayle toward the dance floor. "Or sex." Evelyn's grin was wide and wicked. Gayle shivered again, recalling the explicit scene of near-sex she'd witnessed behind the curtain under the steps earlier.

Evelyn turned and backed into the undulating group of dancers, wigging her hips and crooking both her index fingers. "Come on," she mouthed. The music shifted from loud and annoying to louder and sexy. Gayle sighed and dove into her new life, wondering just how this whole thing might turn out and not really caring at the same time.

Chapter Seven

Look up and to the left.

Noah glanced up from his phone screen and to the left across the jam-packed upper balcony of the club, and saw his friend waving. He sighed, squared his shoulders and focused straight ahead, making his way through the throng. This was not his idea. He didn't even want to be here. But Jake had insisted and he'd made a compelling you-need-to-get-off-your-ass-and-get-laid argument, even as he more or less guaranteed that getting laid was a stone-cold lock if he partied at Nexus.

At least two women hesitated right in front of him, only moving aside with reluctance when he smiled and motioned he was on his way elsewhere. One of them grazed his arm with her half-exposed boob, which gave him a bit of a pleasant shock, but he kept moving, figuring if this was how the first ten minutes went, he'd be set in an hour or two.

"Yo, dude, about time!" His buddy handed him a brown bottle. "Drink up. You're behind."

Noah sniffed the mouth of the bottle, then sipped, hoping his friend knew him well enough by now not to offer him a macro-brew. He did, apparently, so Noah drained half the hoppy IPA in one long gulp. He had come here with the whole getting-laid-already thing in the forefront of his brain, but he knew he had to lubricate his mind first.

"Check it out," Jake said, jamming him in the side with his elbow. "Six o'clock. Couple-a MILFs, if I'm not mistaken. Right up your alley, eh, bro?"

"Fuck you," Noah mumbled around the mouth of the bottle, scanning the crowd for a waitress. He needed at least two more of these things if he was going to venture anywhere near a woman. But he looked where his friend had indicated, if for no other reason than to have somewhere pleasant to rest his gaze while he waited for his beer. One of the women had long blonde hair tumbling down her back. The other one's face was mostly hidden by the sleek, straight fall of her brown hair. Intrigued, he shifted to his left to try to get a better look at them.

He was interrupted by the arrival of his beer and his friend, who'd snagged a couple of chicks into their small conversational circle. He smiled at the women – just girls in their twenties, really, not his type – and sipped, angling for a better view of the MILF table.

"Let's go dance," one of the girls trilled, grabbing his arm. He pulled away from her, intent on making eye contact with a woman across the room. Something about the one with the straight brown hair was making him anxious, as if he knew her or something, which seemed unlikely.

"Maybe later, thanks." He raised an eyebrow at his friend, indicating the other man should take advantage of the Jake-sandwich option. His friend shot him a jaunty salute, then held out both elbows for and led them toward the stairs. He leaned on the wall-height bar and sipped, content to simply observe the two attractive older women, who appeared to be locked in a bit of an emotional exchange.

After about fifteen minutes, they were both leaning on the railing and looking down at the dance floor when the brown-haired one stared right at him, making him blink fast.

Good Christ in a sidecar. It's her.

He held the woman's gaze, unable to stop looking at her even if he wanted to — a familiar place for him, since he'd been visualizing her for the last month or so. More precisely, she — the woman sitting not twenty yards away and glaring at him — had been the superstar of his most vivid and slightly sticky fantasies for the last month or so.

It was fairly clear she remembered him too. At least that was what Noah told himself. He took as casual a sip as he could manage while he waited for her to break their stare-down. She did, of course. He was a pro at this kind of thing. The unlikely, happy coincidence of the incredible woman from the yoga studio being here, tonight, filled his chest and his head, making him wobbly on his feet.

He motioned for a waitress and placed an order for two chilled shots of Chopin vodka, each with a fresh squeeze of lemon, delivered to their table. A bold move, but one he had to make if for no other reason to get her to look up at him. He'd give his left nut to see those incredible green eyes again.

He grinned around the mouth of his bottle when the shots arrived and she did what he'd hoped. He was struck breathless by the intensity of her stare—it spiraled him straight back to the moment when she'd marched out of the yoga room in her miniscule get-up and glared at him until he got back to work. The memory of her—tall, slim yet fit, hair yanked back in a severe ponytail with her somewhat odd-colored eyes boring into him—was etched onto his retinas as if from acid. But it didn't exactly burn in a bad way.

Her full, red lips turned up in a small smile at him before she handed her blonde friend a shot, clinked and knocked it back like a pro. The hairs on Noah's arms stood up and his scalp tingled. Luckily, he was enough of a grown man not to pop a woody in public, but he had to concentrate to keep it from happening. When she glanced at him again, he raised an eyebrow, shrugged and turned away, lest he lose his cool and run over to beg her to leave this noisy chaos with him.

Her companion rose, which drew his—and a lot of other—eyes. The blonde was built like a brick shithouse, to put it mildly, and she was dressed to show it off. When Noah's dream woman joined her, the two of them looked like a pair of models. Between Blondie's killer curves and Yoga Lady's slim, long-legged perfection, they made every single red-blooded male on the balcony turn when they made their way to the steps, pausing at the top to exchange comments and laughter, then descending into the mosh pit of humanity below.

Noah sidled over to the railing so he could keep her in his sights. When she hesitated on the edge of the crowded dance floor, he wanted to run down and tell her he didn't want to jump into the sweaty fray either and she should come with him someplace quiet where they could drink and talk.

But of course, he didn't.

Blondie turned and did an impressive hip shimmy, backward, into the press of bodies, crooking her fingers at her friend. He leaned farther over the railing, willing her to resist. He swore to himself that if she did, if she turned away from the dancing, he would leap over the side — or at least run as fast as he could down the steps — and scoop her up. The waitress brought him his fourth and final beer, which distracted him just long enough for him to lose sight of them both.

"Fuck," he muttered. Spotting the two ladies dressed as they were in that crowd of mostly silver and black would be the proverbial needle in a haystack. He propped himself on his elbows and tried, nonetheless, leaving his beer untouched for a few minutes until he gave up with a louder curse.

"Hey, there he is!" He winced at the sound of Jake's voice. "Come on, man. We've been invited to a private party."

"Not interested," he said, putting the bottle to his lips and taking a long drink.

"We don't have to go anywhere. It's just downstairs." He leaned into Noah's ear, breathing whisky fumes into his face. "Come with me, just to check it out. Please? One of those hotties over there won't take me unless you come too." Jake jerked his chin to their left. Noah spotted the women Jake had left with earlier. He squinted, trying to figure out if a quick fuck with one of them might take his edge off. When one of them, the taller of the two, with thick brown curls and a huge rack, blew him a kiss, he made his decision.

"Fine. But if I don't like the scene, I'm leaving, got it?"

"Got it." He nudged Noah's side. "That one's got the hot 'n readies for you, my friend. He waved at the brunette, who was now licking her lips like a bad porn star. But she did look pretty good doing it. God, he was weak. But still…he needed this, maybe. It would help his mood, maybe. "Her name's Amber," Jake said, filling Noah's nose with brown liquor fumes again.

"Of course it is," he said with a sigh and followed his friend to the women, then down the stairs, around the dance floor where he assumed his real dream woman was having a grand old time, and through a set of double wooden doors behind the DJ. A cool puff of air hit his face, which was a relief after the heat of the main room. He took a step forward into the low-lit room and met with a hand to his chest.

"Hold up, buddy. Twenty bucks. Cash only."

"But…" He tried to see Jake, but he'd disappeared into the gloom along with the chick who obviously shilled for this fucking place, blowing kisses and licking her damn lips at any fool who'd follow her. He didn't have twenty to spare, but he'd come this far, might as well see what was what. He'd never find Yoga Lady out there, anyway. He handed the goon in a suit a twenty, then made his way farther into the room.

Once his eyes adjusted, he saw what appeared to be a repeat of the action outside, only with less overhead lighting. There was a large, seemingly clear acrylic bar staffed by half a dozen women and a couple of guys. Waitress types moved around the clumps of small tables. Music played loud enough to cover most conversations but not loud enough to deafen. The biggest difference his brain finally absorbed was that the women who were sitting, chatting, drinking and flirting were dressed in just enough for it not to be a strip bar.

He eased farther into the room, hugging the perimeter and observing. The women were good-looking, of course, worthy of his twenty bucks' admission. He berated himself, thinking this would have been anything but some kind of a money grab for hapless, dateless, non-dancing dumb-asses. He finally caught sight of Jake. The guy was settled into a chair with a girl who was not the Amber-bait leaning close to him, her boobs spilling out from under a tacky crop-top. Jake was, of course, mesmerized. The guy was an easy mark for shit like this. Of Amber, there was no sign. She must be back outside, blowing kissing to lunkheads and luring them to the 'private party'.

Noah sighed and stuck his fingers in his jeans pockets. He looked around a bit more, noting how close the women would get, but also noting there was a clear line of demarcation. Wondering for a hot second how much more it would cost to the get the full lap dance, he headed for the bar, ready to break his four-beers-and-done rule for the night. His head still spun from the memory of her eyes, her hair and that incredible body in the god damned tiny, yet perfect silver dress. His Yoga Lady…

He sighed and leaned forward, ordered a local IPA, flirted half-heartedly with a couple of the planted, half-dressed chicks until they gave up on him. When he turned and leaned backwards on the bar top, determined to at least get a few voyeuristic jollies for his twenty, he saw Jake had disappeared. Not terribly surprising, since the guy was nothing if not direct when it came to women and what he wanted from them.

Noah put the bottle to his lips and was shocked to find the thing already empty.

Deciding he should do his friendly duty and figure out where the guy was, just in case this was a shake-down joint on top of everything else, he moved through the crowd, deflecting the women and keeping his eyes on a couple of doorways covered in black, flowy material, like curtains. The high, lilting laughter coupled with low, masculine chuckles and utterances he couldn't make out all the way through the room. When he got to one of the doorways, another suit stopped him. Big surprise.

"Sorry, pal. You don't come back here without an escort."

"Good name for it," he said. "I'm trying to find my friend. To let him know I'm leaving."

This seemed to perk the bouncer guy up. "Hey, don't go yet. You just got here." He made a subtle motion with one hand and a couple of girls materialized as if conjured from thin air. Noah sighed at the sad dreariness of the whole scene and the girls looped their arms into his and guided him toward a table.

"I'm not interested, ladies. Really." One of them gave him a not-too-gentle shove into a chair, then giggled to her friend before turning to face him. She was older than most of the companions, which piqued his waning interest. She had long, jet-black hair and startling blue eyes which seemed to bore into him, as if reading his reluctance and willing him to think differently. She smiled, slowly, and put her hands on the chair arms where he sat, pinning his wrists and giving him an unadulterated view of her tits. They were not huge, but not small either and tipped with dark, rock-hard nipples... *Just right*, he thought with a wry smile, releasing the big-boy control he'd kept over himself, groaning under his breath when his dick hardened, trapped as is was under too-tight jeans. He tried to move his arms to reach for her, but she kept pressing down, letting him leer all he wanted, but not touch.

Another hand landed on his thigh, making him flinch. "We get to touch," the woman whispered, giving him a face full of spearmint fumes and a whiff of booze.

"Really," he said, not moving as the other woman's hand reached the point where his jeans were strained by his erection. "Seems a bit unfair."

"You are fucking adorable," the woman still looming over him said. "How old are you anyway? I didn't know they went for fake IDs at the door of this place." Her lips found his earlobe. Then her teeth, which made him shiver and clench his jaw against the need to either shove her and handsy-chick off him or throw the talkative one on the table and fuck her silly in front of an audience.

Wouldn't be the first time, after all.

That memory, of a life he'd led briefly in sheer desperation, made his body soften ever so slightly in shame. He looked away from her tits and focused on the ceiling above them.

"Well?"

"Well, what? Well, will I pay yet more money to disappear behind the curtain with you so you can do whatever it is I can afford, or, well, how did I get in here in the first place?" He leveled his gaze at her, giving her his best I-don't-give-a-damn expression.

"Both," she said, with a grin before standing up, taking his hand, turning away from him but putting his palm on her shoulder so he'd follow her. "But later. I want to get a closer look at you first."

Noah's eyes were drawn to her ass, which was barely covered in a pair of black shorts, her legs, which were long and lean, and the sky-high black heels she wore as if they were a pair of sneakers. He made it as far as the curtain, saw the grinning bouncer with his hand out, then stopped. His date or whatever she was turned around, annoyance clear in her eyes. But he took her hand, yanked her close, put his lips to her ear and whispered, "I'm twenty-nine but look ten years younger. It's a blessing and a curse." She tried to pull away and grab his hand again, but he held on tight, one hand in the small of her back, the other copping a feel of her breast. She sighed and leaned into him, giving new life to his softening erection. "I thank you kindly for your interest, but I can't afford any more direct attention, if you know what I mean. I'm just a poor working man. I don't have spare dough for this." He caught her earlobe in his teeth, giving her the same hard bite she'd given him.

Her nipple hardened under his thumb.

He smelled her lust curling around them, beckoning him further.

Well, at least I know I've still got it. Thought I might have lost my edge.

He took her hand again, kissed it like some kind of a gallant knight, shifted his dick with a wince and a wink then turned away and headed for the doors. This was not what he wanted. Not anymore.

He wanted his Yoga Lady. And, by God, he was going back out there to find her.

Chapter Eight

The full force of the heat and ear-shattering music hit him hard, but he moved past the DJ booth and plunged into the crowd. He felt strong and powerful, dancing with first one, then another, then another stranger while he kept his eyes peeled for his target. One thing Noah knew how to do was dance. He'd made plenty of money doing it both on stage and off for a several years when he'd dropped out of college, only a semester shy of his degree. But he'd avoided it the last few, hoping that by coming home to Grand Rapids and dealing directly with his father's failing business he could forget all the glorious, horrible, wonderful ignominy of those lost years.

He'd dealt with it all right. The utter failure of it had ruined his parents' marriage, sending his mother fleeing to Florida and his father to a too-early grave, which had left Noah with little choice but to take the odd construction or landscaping job for the past two years. He sought to be inspired by something — anything — again.

He'd yet to find it, at least on the employment front. He'd been living small off his savings from his dancer-escort days, banking the most he could of whatever he got paid for odd jobs that kept him outdoors as much as he could manage. In the interim, he'd gotten hooked on craft beer — something super easy to do in this town swimming in the stuff, with nationally and internationally famous breweries bracketing all the smaller pubs and tasting rooms scattered east to west.

As he ground against one very hot woman while looking over her shoulder the whole time for another, he realized he had found yet another layer to the rock bottom of his life. His dance partner ran her fingers around the back of his neck and into his hair, rubbing her tits against his chest and letting him shove his thigh between hers. The music was an endless loop of thumping, erotic noise. Noah tried to enjoy what he was doing — the sensation of the woman's hips under his hands, the unmistakable heat of her pussy on his leg, the soft press of her body along his. But his mind wouldn't connect with it somehow. It wouldn't let go of his seemingly new and urgent prime directive — *find Yoga Lady. Find her now. Dance, drink, flirt but get her away from here so I can really get to know her.*

Ridiculous.

She was probably happily married and out with her girlfriend who was fighting with her husband so they were determined to live a little — to do their own flirting and grinding and drinking then leave. She would have little to no interest in him. A wanna-be but never-have-been landscape architect, destined to run his father's successful business that had gone completely bankrupt thanks to a string of shitty life choices. A not-so-failed male stripper and escort. A construction grunt. *The faceless guy who mows the lawn and mulches the flower beds.*

He had recently lucked into something new. Something that would take him into the beer business, so at least he had it to look forward to. It didn't pay much, but he'd still keep his landscaping jobs for ready cash. It could be a fresh start for him. A dare-he-think-it career in something he enjoyed. Even if he would never, ever enjoy anything as much as he did working outdoors — planting things, teaching people how to treat the things he'd planted, planning elaborate gardens, patios and other outdoor spaces.

But it was a no-go for him, other than being that guy — the one who mowed the lawn and mulched.

As he snapped back to himself, he smiled at the woman, who was leaning in to him, anticipating a kiss. "Thanks," he said, and disentangled himself before slipping in between some of the undulating bodies by way of escape. Noah didn't kiss. It was something drilled into him, and hard, by Drake, the guy who'd trained him as a dancer, then pimped him out on the side.

'You catch things when you kiss. Things like clingy women. Women equate kissing with love and we are not in the business of love. Just the business of fantasy, and of sex, of course, should that be required.'

Noah had kissed a few of the women, of course. How could he not? And sure enough, each time but for one he'd had to be moved to another district because the woman in question would demand him every time, sometimes more than twice a week, which was not how Drake ran his show. His stable of men were not in the business of making connections. They swooped in, played the requested fantasy and swooped out, never to be seen or heard from again.

Noah had seen a lot of California — L.A. first, and San Diego, then San Fran, then NoCal. He'd danced and flirted and, at times, fucked his way into the history books, if those books were to record the relative popularity of a certain young man who looked younger than he was and had become a serious expert in all of the above. His name during those years had not been Noah. It had been something else. Something he no longer wished to recall.

He wove his way in and around the dancers, taking the odd moment to slide up to a woman in a sexy silver dress only to determine it wasn't her. He copped plenty of feels and had his own junk stroked, squeezed and otherwise admired through his jeans as he went. But the longer he worked through the crowd, the more he believed he'd never find her, and if he did, she'd either laugh in his face or ignore him.

After what was probably about an hour but felt like three, he squeezed his way out and onto the perimeter again. He was barely winded and only the lightest sheen of sweat had broken out on his forehead. He swiped at it and grabbed a water bottle off a passing tray, winking at the waitress when she protested. Leaning against another wall-height bar ledge, he sucked back the hydration in two long gulps, then tossed the empty onto yet another passing tray.

The damn place had gotten even more crowded and annoying while he'd been on the hunt for Yoga Lady. Women and men, all attractive, all smiling, all holding bottles and glasses, moved around him. But he kept his gaze trained on the one corner of the dancers he could still see. Now he knew about the 'private party' option, he spotted the girls acting as bait, luring single guys out away from the dance floor and bar and around behind the DJ. He fought off the temptation to give it another go, as worked up and horny as he was from all the bumping and grinding.

But the thought of an anonymous fuck, even in the name of taking off his very sharp edge, didn't really appeal. He was the king of the anonymous fuck, or he had been, and he wanted to leave it behind him. He wanted to find Yoga Lady. But it seemed as though that would have to remain in the realm of his own fevered fantasy. Not for lack of trying on his part. Besides, he had a long day of yard work tomorrow and Sunday, plus he was starting his new job on Monday—a salesman, or 'brand ambassador' as they called it in the biz, for one of the biggest, most successful Grand Rapids-based breweries. Could be fun, or at least more interesting than installing ceiling tiles outside a yoga studio.

After leaving a quick text for Jake letting him know he was headed home, thanking him for the invite and wishing his best for disease-free girls, he headed around the dance floor, his mind awash with frustration. Deciding to take a quick piss before stepping outside and calling for a ride share, he made a detour, which took him under the spiral steps up to the balcony where he'd begun this stupid night. A clump of people blocked him at first—one couple drunkenly arguing, another in a serious lip-lock and a third that seemed to be... Noah froze, taking in the vision of the third couple.

The woman was pressed back against the wall. The man loomed over her, one hand on the wall over her head, the other seemingly keeping her wrists held in place behind her. Her face was tilted up to his. When their lips met, Noah shivered and moved back, embarrassed but wanting to make sure it was her — his Yoga Lady — making out under the steps. The kiss was long but somewhat unsexy. Noah knew sexy when it came to kissing and this was not it. The guy dropped the hand he had propped on the wall and wrapped his long fingers around the back of her neck, which meant she was more or less held hostage by him.

Noah's hackles rose the more he watched her manage to break her wrists free at one point and place them on the guy's ample chest. But he kept kissing her and when she wrapped her arms around his neck, Noah felt utterly defeated. If Yoga Lady was stepping out on her no-doubt rich-as-fuck hubs, she was doing it up right. The guy was young, hot and eager, that much was clear.

He slumped back against the wall, pissed at himself for even coming this way now. A distinctly unhappy sound hit his ears, making him lurch forward again and take in the scene. This time, tall, hot 'n eager had one hand up her short dress, heading north in a way that did not seem to please her. He retreated, still kissing her, then put his hand between her legs. Noah saw his forearm flex and heard her yelp of surprised pain.

She yanked herself away from him with some effort, leaving them staring at each other for a few seconds, both of them breathing heavily. Noah's hands curled into fists and he studied the other man's taller but slimmer-than-his physique, seeking weaknesses and deciding where he'd punch the handsy fucker first. Yoga Lady smoothed her hair and took a step back from him, looking over his shoulder as if trying to find someone. Noah ducked into the shadow, not willing to give away his position just yet.

The guy smiled and ran a finger down her flushed cheek, across her bare shoulder, down her arm and up to her boob. She slapped him, hard and loud enough for everyone under the stairs to startle and look at them.

"Fucking bitch," the guy growled, making a lunge for her at the same instant Noah placed himself firmly between them, pushing the guy away with one hand while putting his other arm back, shielding her.

"I think the lady was pretty clear your presence is no longer desired," he said, keeping his voice mild and conversational. He sensed her slipping away from him, likely into one of the curtained-off side rooms where God knew what she'd find. But he kept his gaze on Mr. Touchy-Feely, hoping this wouldn't end in a brawl that would get him kicked out of here or worse.

The dude was pretty drunk, that much was clear—he swayed forward, then back, his eyes glazing over. "Dude, I wasn't gonna... Oh fuck it." He waved a hand in Noah's general direction, then staggered out from under the steps, leaving Noah standing with one arm outstretched to nothing.

He turned, praying she hadn't bolted yet. All he wanted to know at this point was her name.

He slid behind the black velvet barrier and tried to find her in the scrum of couples in various stages of making out and, in a few cases, actual, awkward, half-dressed sex. Sad, he thought. He pushed past them, desperate and eager in equal measure. He was damn glad he never had to hook up in some half-assed brothel posing as a dance club.

When he finally emerged at the back of the hallway full of moaning and groaning and dampness, he saw her crouched down to her ankles, her arms wrapped around her legs, her face pressed into her knees.

He sat in front of her, put his hand on the back of her head, and waited. When she lifted her face, it was tear streaked, her eyes bloodshot, her face twisted into a frown. "Who *are* you?" she demanded, pulling away slightly. "I mean, I know who you are. But not…I mean. Oh, fuck it." She stood, her hand to her neck. Panic suffused her expression. "Oh shit. I…I lost it." She grabbed both his arms and gripped tight. "You have to help me find it."

"Okay," he said, loving the feel of her hands on him, despite her panicked condition. "What did you lose?"

"My…my necklace."

Noah looked around their feet, hoping she hadn't lost it on the dance floor. If so, she might as well forget it forever. "Okay," he repeated, for lack of anything better.

"Where's Evelyn?" Yoga Lady still had her fingertips dug into his biceps, but he didn't care. She could hang on to him forever as far as he was concerned. He cupped her elbows. Her skin was ice cold to his touch. "Can you find her?"

She wasn't drunk, best he could tell, but she was shivering so hard her teeth chattered. He used that excuse to tuck her under his arm and relish the closeness and warmth of her body against his.

Craven, Noah. But awfully nice.

She put one arm around his waist and let him lead her back through the sad-sack orgy in the hall and into the main room. "Who's Evelyn?"

"She was with me. You bought us the vodka shots."

"Oh right, the blonde."

He cast his eyes around, hoping to drag out this moment so she could stay close to him, under his protection, and Evelyn, the blonde ran up to them, her phone in her hand. "Thank God, there you are."

"Yes, here I am," Yoga Lady, whose name he really ought to learn, said.

Evelyn eyeballed him in a way that made him feel like a naughty teenager. Luckily, he loved it when strong women acted on their strength, so he was the opposite of intimidated. He pulled Yoga Lady closer. "Who the hell are you?" she demanded, taking her friend's hand and dragging her out from under his arm. "And what are you doing?"

"He's fine," Yoga Lady insisted with a sniffle, her hand still at her neck. "He got rid of some creep for me. But Evelyn... I lost my necklace. With the ring."

"Nope. I have it. It must have slipped off in the bathroom. I saw it on the floor."

"Thank God." She held out her hand and Evelyn dropped a heavy silver chain with a what looked like a ring into it. His dream woman pressed the ring to her lips and closed her eyes.

Evelyn treated him to a hairy eyeball, since he was lurking with no real purpose anymore. He turned to Yoga Lady and held out his hand. "Here. Let me."

She met his gaze, which almost brought him to his knees—he'd been dreaming about those eyes for so long. She frowned, looked down at the necklace in her hand, then held it out to him. Evelyn sucked in a breath but didn't say anything when Yoga Lady turned and lifted her incredible fall of sleek brown hair, exposing the nape of her neck to him. He gulped, then focused on the complex clasp for a few seconds.

He draped the thing around her neck and after only a few fumbles, managed to work the connection. His entire being seemed centered on the bit of her vulnerable flesh under her hair before she let it fall. He touched it without thinking, then jerked his hand away, realizing the inappropriateness of it, although he'd treasure its silken perfection for days.

"Okay, fine. Great. Let's get the hell out of here," Evelyn said from somewhere behind him.

Yoga Lady turned and met his gaze. Her green eyes were steady, her lips pursed, indicating she was confused by him. He reached out and took her hand, lowered his lips to it then let it go. She smiled — a crooked, adorable thing he loved already.

Dear God, but I am smacked upside the head by this woman. Why? What makes her so fucking special?

Evelyn took her hand and tugged her away from him. She seemed reluctant to go. But her friend was insistent and, given the general vibe of this place, he didn't blame her. He watched them as if from a long way away, only thinking to ask at the last minute, "Hey, wait. What's your name?"

Evelyn frowned over her shoulder at him. Yoga Lady stopped and turned to face him, arms crossed like she'd done that morning at the studio. He walked closer. "I'm Noah. Noah Stokes," he said, holding out his hand, willing her to take it. If he could just know her name, he felt he might survive the next few weeks.

She opened her mouth, but her friend grabbed her arm and pulled her away. "Our ride's here. Sorry, kid," she said. "Gotta go."

He left his hand outstretched as they made for the front door, still feeling her hair, still seeing the sweet spot of her neck she'd given him access to, if only for a brief moment. Finally, he stuck his fingers back in his pockets and waited a few beats, giving them time to find their ride before making his way to the door.

Chapter Nine

"Yo! Stokes! God damn, boy, you're gonna get yourself killed."

Noah flinched when something hit the back of his head. "What the fuck?" He whirled to face his assailant, who stood with his gloved hands on his hips and a smirk playing around his mouth. "I was working."

"You were daydreaming. And that thing you're holding will slice off your fuckin' foot if you're not more careful."

Noah flipped the guy off and got back to work. He had been drifting. But he was also exhausted, which didn't help. After stumbling into his apartment Friday night, he'd been disappointed to discover he was wound up on too many levels to sleep. Every square inch of his skin seemed to crawl. His ears rang. His legs were restless.

And of course, he was hornier than a boatload of sailors.

Celibacy did not agree with him. Not one bit. But he'd endured it as a sort of detox from his old life in California and up to this exact point, it hadn't been a real hardship. But the night before, it had been exactly that.

And had only gotten harder.

He'd tried everything — cold shower, hot shower, ten miles on the stationary bike in the corner of his small space, huge glass of bourbon — and all these things after he'd jacked off not once, but twice, to the thought of pressing his too-eager lips to the back of Yoga Lady's neck. It had been maddening and frustrating. And he still couldn't even manage an hour or so of fitful dozing before he had to get up and meet his crew for a long day of yard maintenance.

He wiped the sweat off his forehead with the bandana he kept in his back pocket, pissed that his hand shook as if he had the world's worst hangover. He supposed he did, in a way. A Yoga Lady hangover, perhaps. Whatever it was, it was damn close to killing him. He had to let it go. But he had no idea how to do it. Everywhere he looked he could see some part of her — either in her sexy dress, or in her minimal exercise gear. Her eyes, her lips, the set of her jaw, the fall of her hair, the length of her legs — he was obsessed beyond all reason.

Plus, he was still convinced she was married to some rich asshole and had only been playing out of school the night before, getting back at him for some ill-chosen tumble at a convention with a stranger or a quick-and-ugly with his secretary. Men still did that. He'd know. Half of the women he'd serviced in his former life confessed they were only doing it to get back at their husbands.

God, man. Get a grip already. Get two. They're on sale.

For the next three hours, Noah went about his assigned business — weeding gardens, trimming hedges, blowing grass clippings off sidewalks. But his mind never left the long, porcelain line of her neck, the deep red of her short fingernails, the raw panic in her eyes over the necklace which had held what looked like a man's wedding ring.

Something about that memory made him pause, mid-clip. He stood, the dangerously sharp tool he used gaping open, along with his mouth. Realizing this before the crew boss caught him again, he closed the shears around the green frond destined for death, then went on down the row, opening and closing the thing without even paying close attention to what he was clipping off.

He finished and did a quick phone check behind the truck. This particular boss had a thing about the guys always 'chasing pussy on their phones' as he put it, rather poetically, Noah thought. Which meant he couldn't afford to get caught looking at his, since he'd already taken a water bottle to the back of his head earlier. He had another thirty-five minutes to his shift so he found some make-work he could do without thinking, spreading the last of the mulch around some trees and shrubs. The minute he was able, he jumped behind the wheel of his third-hand truck, plugged his phone into the cigarette lighter charger and did an internet search for something that had hit him like the proverbial bolt of lightning earlier.

Once he'd figured out who the hot, if somewhat bossy blonde had been — Evelyn Fitzgerald, the woman who would technically be his boss come Monday — he'd had a quick flash of insight combined with a random memory and realized just who his mystery Yoga Lady might be. It only took a couple of minutes to find what he was seeking. He held on to the wheel with one hand and thumb-scrolled down an article titled *Beer and Wine Distribution Mogul, Entrepreneur, Philanthropist Ethan Connolly Dies in Private Plane Crash over Texas.*

He'd had a few widows on his client list—women who began as regulars to the bar where he danced who'd actually been among the first in line for his direct attention, once Drake had determined him ready for such a thing. One in particular had been in what she called the 'early stages of grief', which had not, if he remembered correctly, damped her libido one iota. If anything, she'd been insatiable.

But those had been early, heady days of his life as…whatever the fuck he wanted to call it. He'd been called a male escort, gigolo, Bringer of Extreme Fantasy with Happy Endings…but he'd been a common prostitute. He'd taken money—an inordinate amount of it—in exchange for having sex, paid a portion of it to his pimp and pocketed the rest.

Sweat clouded his vision and his phone screen went dark when he tried to muscle past the fury rising in his throat at the thought of himself then. One thing he did recall about his horny widows—they sometimes wore their dead husbands' rings on necklaces. Just like Yoga Lady had done the night before. He'd put the thing back on her himself.

Which had brought him here—reading about Yoga Lady's dead husband in an article from almost three years ago. He'd been in California when it had happened, at rock bottom after getting busted for possession of way too many bottles of prescription pain killers and summarily fired from his bar dancing job.

He'd been so sick of having sex with strangers for money he'd been methodically collecting the pills from the medicine chests of his various 'clients' with a serious eye towards chasing every single one of them with a liter of Jack Daniels on the beach.

Something in him had made that strange connection and sure enough, there she was in a photo, dressed in something incredible and no-doubt designer, on the arm of her tall, gray-haired, slim and super-handsome hubby. Dear Jesus, but she was a goddess, an exquisite picture of feminine perfection to his eye—strong, smart, savvy, fit, tall—all his favorite things in a woman.

She was obviously in mourning for a man who'd been almost fifteen years her senior, wealthier than God, never been married, and, according to one of his many rich and famous friend quoted in this Wall Street Journal article, never happier than when he'd met and wooed the young saleswoman in his San Francisco-based distributorship. Noah wiped his eyes free of sweat and touched the phone screen again, eager for more details.

Gayle.

Yoga Lady had a name and he'd found it.

Gayle Jackson Connolly.

Noah sat in the stifling hot truck for so long, scrolling around and finding out as much as he could of her horrific personal tragedy, that when he looked up, the rest of the crew had gone and the owner of the obnoxious McMansion where he'd been working was glaring at him suspiciously from her front door. He gave her a friendly wave with a shaking hand, thanks to the heat and his lack of food intake in the last half a day, before firing up the rebuilt engine and driving out of the gated neighborhood toward his apartment.

He ate two bananas and downed nearly a gallon of Gatorade standing in his kitchen, phone in his other hand, eyes darting down the screen, reading yet more about his new obsession. When, after reading through an industry-based article about the crash, he realized that Ethan wasn't the only Connolly to be killed, his hand shook so hard he dropped the device and slid down the cabinet until he was sitting on the cracked linoleum, staring into space.

Finally, he got control of himself, picked the phone up and did one final search for 'Gayle Connolly' in recent beer-industry press.

"Bingo," he whispered. He read through the information, his eyes widening in shock when he had to accept he might just be running into the beautiful, tragic Gayle a lot sooner than she might think.

Chapter Ten

Monday morning couldn't come quickly enough. Gayle had spent the weekend huddled under a blanket, reliving the huge mistake of Friday night's adventure even while her mind wouldn't let go of the memory of the kid from the construction lift outside her yoga studio – he'd been at the dance club, of all the places in the city he might've materialized. It confounded her, which was nothing compared to her confusion about how calm and protected he'd made her feel for a split second.

When Evelyn had pulled her away, she'd been half inclined to throw herself at him, to beg him to put his arm around her again. Or, worse, to touch her shoulder the way he had after re-fastening her necklace.

Dear God, but she was a sap. She should've just let the drunk guy she'd been making out with do what he'd wanted. That would've driven all thoughts of being a sexually whole woman again right out of her brain, and how. But the second he'd reached between her legs and actually touched her, it seemed a negative electric shock had flown through her body. She'd wanted to throw up, frankly. But instead she'd slapped his stupid face.

Ugh. She hated herself by the time Monday morning finally arrived. But thankfully she had a long, challenging week ahead—just the thing for forgetting how she'd behaved Friday night. She'd barely even been able to talk to Evelyn on Saturday, she'd been so mortified by herself.

"Honey, please *do not* worry," her friend had reassured her, repeatedly. "It was your first outing. We'll do it better next time."

"Trust me, Evelyn. There will never be a next time. I'm not cut out for…"

"Fun? A life? Please, Gayle."

"I don't know. I was…it was…I don't know anymore. But thank God you were there, especially when I lost my damn necklace."

"Yes, well…"

Gayle had snapped to, recalling that Evelyn had her own issues going on at the moment. "So, have you talked to him?"

"Of course. The damn man was home when I got there."

"Home? I thought he was in Denver."

"He turned around and came back." Evelyn had sighed and Gayle had sensed a thick curl of jealous smoke enter her consciousness. "Silly man. But we kissed and made up."

"Good," Gayle had said, not wanting to hear anymore lest she say something rude and inappropriate. "I'm glad for you both. Gonna go now, hon. Enjoy your weekend." She'd hung up without letting the other woman say anything else and sat for a long time, the phone pressed to her forehead, her jaw clenched in an effort not to scream.

But finally, Monday morning arrived, as it always did. She rose at five, ran six miles in the already warm morning through her old neighborhood, showered and grabbed coffee. Realizing she'd be sitting at her desk a solid hour before most people even got up, she smiled at herself in the rearview mirror. But it was a grim smile.

So what? I'm entitled. I tried to act like a regular person and go out for drinks and dancing and almost lost my mind. Obviously, I am no longer a regular person.

She jammed the car into reverse, then squealed her way down the quiet road toward the only thing she knew how to do anymore — work.

By the weekly nine-thirty a.m. all-hands sales meeting, she'd gotten so many things ticked off her to-do list, she figured she should make a point to be in the office by seven every day. "I emailed you my latest spreadsheet with corrections," she said to her assistant with a quick smile. "Would you tidy it up for me, so I can present it at Thursday's management lunch?"

"Sure thing," the woman said. "Oh, and Gayle…"

She turned, her mind already on the meeting ahead, since she'd be announcing the breweries getting slashed from her book for good. "Hmm?" She checked her tablet distractedly.

"Someone sent this for you." Gayle looked at the woman, who was pointing to a huge bouquet of summer flowers on the table between a set of chairs where people sat when they were waiting to see her. "Here's the card. Your door was closed when they got delivered so…" The woman's voice trailed away. Gayle frowned and took the square envelope with her name fake hand-written on it. She glanced at the woman — *Susan, God damn it. Her name is Susan* — before ripping it open and staring at the words a few seconds before they settled into her brain.

Dear Gayle, I swear I'm not a stalker, but I would love to buy you a coffee, or a beer, or a water sometime and talk. I hope you don't take this the wrong way. I will see you soon. Noah (a.k.a. Yoga Window Guy)

Once she'd read the words for a sixth time, her mind accepted what she'd known the second she saw the flowers. Noah, the cute, young, construction worker guy-slash-hero-from-the-nightclub, was not going away anytime soon. To her surprise, she was smiling by the time she tucked the note into her leather portfolio, which currently housed the bad news for a fair number of breweries in their market. When she met Susan's eyes, the other woman was smiling too. Gayle's face flushed hot and she tried not to run out of her office door toward the conference room.

Taking a deep breath to center herself and get straight in her head that today was about work, not a ridiculous flirtation with some…kid who knew how to call a florist, she pushed open the door and walked into the half-filled room. She'd always run great meetings — efficient, to the point, useful for anyone who attended and this one had been required for all sales and warehouse staff. She saw the IT people had set up the screen with one of her favorite motivational quotes from Estée Lauder — "I didn't get there by wishing for it or hoping for it, but by working for it" — displayed in large red font. Gayle met the gazes of each man and woman waiting for her and took her seat.

She immediately spotted three people were missing, which aggravated her, but there were still three minutes to go before the official start. A few people asked after her weekend. A few others asked how she was settling back into life in Michigan. Most people averted their gazes. It was amazing how being the object of such ongoing sympathy after tragedy changed the way people treated her — as if she had a contagious disease, or as if her bad luck in life would rub off on them if they got too friendly.

But it was all fine and dandy with her. She wasn't here to make buddies. There was work to be done and she'd been hired to do it. Ben ducked into the room and sat at the far end of the table, after giving her a small wave. The other three missing staff — two sales people and the warehouse manager — finally honored the rest of them with their presences. Gayle swallowed the urge to snap at them and glanced down at the chart she'd prepared for the AV portion of the meeting. A corner of the card from the flowers caught her eye. She touched it, marveling at her ability to let it distract her from these crucial next sixty minutes.

When the conference room door shut behind the last tardy staffer, she looked up and beamed at the room. "Well, guys, you've done it." She waited, letting it sink in. Almost everyone smiled at her blankly. "No, really. You have. You've done it. You've set a record for July sales of craft beer." She touched her screen and the TV screen changed to a chart reflecting the last three years' worth of sales. It did, indeed, show a significant spike in sales from the previous one and a huge jump from two years ago. She gave a slow clap and waited until the room joined her.

The conference room door opened, sending a puff of air-conditioned air into her face. She frowned when someone stepped into the room. "Oh, sorry, Gayle," Ben said. "I had Susan add something last minute to the agenda for this morning. It's my bad. Come on in, Noah."

Gayle's heart actually stopped beating for about a half second. At least, that was what it felt like when she watched the man who'd made her almost break her ankle, who'd pulled her out of her yoga class for reasons she still couldn't parse and who'd rescued her from her ignominious return to a social life on Friday night, look right at her with a half-smile and a shrug of *'I told you I'd see you soon.'*

Her hand went to her throat. But she'd left Ethan's ring draped on its chain on the corner of the mirror over her dresser earlier, figuring she could make it through a workday without worrying it to death. She wanted it now so badly it hurt. The young man's compelling brown gaze hadn't left hers. They were staring at each other like a pair of star-crossed lovers for so long someone had to clear their throat to break up the moment. Gayle flinched at the sound and her gaze flew to Ben, who was looking around the room in confusion.

"Right," she said, before swallowing hard. "Okay. So...Ben. What did you add?" She glanced down at her tablet and saw the addition now. It was something she probably should have noted before walking in here, since the addition had the name *Noah Stokes, new brand ambassador for Fitzgerald Brewing Company*, right on it. "Ah, I see." She smiled in Noah's general direction without looking at him. "So, let's continue, shall we?"

Her voice was high, tight, tense-sounding—weak. And nothing pissed her off more than appearing to be weak.

She frowned at Ben, who shrugged and looked down at his agenda. She frowned at him—at Noah—who smiled, which made a shiver shoot down her spine. She tried to convince herself that it was embarrassment over how they'd last met. But it wasn't and she damn well knew it.

Her portion of the meeting ended after exactly forty minutes in near total silence. She'd dropped some serious bombshells on them in this second round of cuts. A few of the more competent sales people had complained and she'd listened, stating, "If you have a serious argument in favor of keeping an account, make an appointment with my assistant in the next two weeks and make your pitch for them. Please include actual sales numbers and your personal projections for how we can turn them around." She'd met every pair of eyes around the table. "I will consider your well-structured arguments. But not a bunch of bullshit about breweries who give you freebies or treat you like royalty just because." Gayle rarely cursed in the office, so when she did, people sat up and paid attention.

"All right, then, Ben. Would you like to introduce your guest?" The weird squeakiness was back. She cleared her throat again and smiled in Noah's general direction once more.

"I'll let him introduce himself," Ben said with a dismissive wave.

Noah rose to his feet. Gayle kept her gaze fixed on the tablet in front of her even though the temptation to stare at him—to take him in from the top of his dark blond hair down his model-perfect body—was one of the hardest things she'd ever had to resist. "Hi, everyone. I'm Noah and I'll be working with you on behalf of Fitzgerald Brewing. I'm hoping to set a few ride-along days with some of you today."

Gayle watched the five women who were suitably dazzled by him begin to flip their hair and attempt other eye-catching, mating-dance rituals. Her face reddened and her throat closed up so tight she couldn't breathe for a few seconds.

He said a few more things, but she couldn't hear him for the loud ringing in her ears. Finally, the woman sitting next to her, who'd been making goo-goo eyes at the handsome young man as he moved easily around the room, nudged her leg. When Gayle frowned, the woman nodded in the direction of the table which held a full complement of silent people, all of them staring at her, waiting for her to dismiss them. Noah was also sitting, also looking at her, one eyebrow raised in a way that shot her right back the Godawful moment in the yoga studio.

"Right, okay, so. Let's get to it, shall we?" She stood fast and practically ran out of the room and down the hall to the relative safety of her office. Once she got there, after what felt like about an hour's worth of walking, she shut the glass door and leaned back against it, eyes closed, sweat drenching the back of her blouse.

What had just happened? Why did this man keep reappearing in her life? She touched her neck, but the ring still wasn't there. Her fingertips felt ice-cold against the heat of her skin. A phone rang. But it wasn't the one on her desk, or the one in her pocket. It was another one. One from nearly three years ago. The voice on the other end came from a stranger. A stranger telling her the news while she drove home from the office, her mind already on the things she needed to pack. Already looking forward to being reunited with her family, even if it meant an unwanted trip to Disney World.

A sharp rap on the glass behind her made her yelp and jump away from it as if it had burned her. "Um, give me a minute," she called out in the same tight voice she'd been using in the meeting. She stumbled over her own feet, approaching her desk. After putting her tablet and portfolio down, she sucked in a long breath, sipped her cold coffee, then turned to face the door. "Come in." She had one hand on the glass top, the other one gripping her phone.

The door opened slowly, revealing the man she knew would be there, making yet another reappearance in her life. "Hi," he said, standing half in, half out of her office, his hands tucked into the pockets of his khakis. She glared at him. Her legs shook so hard she eased around behind the desk and sat before she fell down.

"Hello," she said, keeping it noncommittal, willing him to leave. "This is certainly a surprise."

"Yes, well...it's a small world."

"So it would seem." She tapped her fingertips on the desk top but didn't say anything else. He matched her silence without making it awkward. His face was a mask of patience—extraordinarily handsome patience. She blew out a breath. "Can I do something for you? I really have a lot to do today."

His slow, easy smile emerged, widening, making her scalp tingle and her ears burn hot. "Did you like the flowers?"

She sighed and rolled her eyes. "Yes. They are nice." More silence. "Thank you."

"You're welcome." He tilted his head. She tried not to react. "And...?"

"And what?" She bit off the ends of the two words, hoping to convey her unhappiness with his continued presence. She stared at him, a bizarre sensation filling all her senses. She could smell, feel, practically taste Ethan right then. She closed her eyes, hating her life so much it made her teeth hurt.

"Gayle?" He was next to her now. She could tell. Warmth rolled off his skin and caressed hers in a way different from what she'd felt with Ethan. "Are you all right?" His hand was on her shoulder. His fingers touched her jaw, her chin, her lips. The heat of him made her feel safe, and loved, and no longer wretchedly alone. She jerked away from him with such violence her chair rolled backward and hit the wall with her still in it. He stood, arms crossed, not talking, not demanding anything of her.

"I'm fine. Please go." She swallowed hard, tears burning their way down her cheeks. "Please?" This last came out a raw, painful whisper. She kept a death grip on the chair arms and her gaze trained down on the floor. "I don't know what you want from me but..."

He crouched down in front of her, his palms covering her hands. "I don't want anything from you," he said, his voice soft. She clenched her jaw, determined not to look at him. But he wouldn't move. "Relax, Gayle. It's all right. I'm sorry—"

"Don't fucking tell me you're fucking sorry," she spat out, finally meeting his eyes. Strands of her hair had escaped her tie-back and hung over her eyes. She must look like a straight-up crazy person. She tried to lean away from him, to pull her hands out from under his, but he wouldn't let her. Instead of being threatening, however, the gesture was the opposite — it was oddly comforting.

"Okay, I won't. I'm not sorry. Fuck sorry." He smiled. His face was so close. His lips so…very tempting.

"Yes. Fuck sorry," she whispered. "I think you can let go of me now." She allowed herself to smile at him and it felt so good, she kept doing it until an inappropriate giggle burst out of her, followed by a loud chuckle and a bark of laughter. Noah leaned back on his heels, hands on his thighs while she had her hysterical fit, both hands clapped over her mouth, tears rolling down her face. "Jesus," she said, waving her hands in front of her eyes. "Wow." She swiped at her cheeks and leaned back. Noah hadn't moved an inch. He sat, watching her. "So, you can go now. For real."

He rose, graceful as a dancer, and tucked his hands back in his pockets. "About that coffee?"

Gayle sighed and stared at the ceiling. "You are persistent."

"Yes, it's one of my many stellar qualities." He waited in silence while she pondered this strange life turn she'd taken. "So, when are we having coffee?"

"I never said I wanted to have coffee with you." *Dear Lord, am I flirting? I am, indeed.* She leveled her gaze at him. "Did I?"

He shrugged and leaned on her desk. "Water? Beer? Wine? Tea?" His grin widened. "I'm flexible as well as persistent."

"Are you even old enough to drink?"

"I'm twenty-nine. I'll be thirty in a few weeks." He ran a hand across his lips and around the back of his neck. "I'm blessed and cursed with a face that's always looked about ten years younger than I actually am."

She scoffed and crossed her arms but was relieved to know he wasn't as young as she'd guessed. "I'm not drinking anything with you." She rose, keeping her hands on the desk top to steady herself. "I don't know what this is, but I don't think I'm…ready to date, if you know what I mean."

"I do know. And I wouldn't exactly call it a date. More like a chat."

Her skin tingled. God help her, he was gorgeous. But she couldn't do this. She wouldn't do this. "No, thanks," she said, refastening her tie-back. "Not interested." She smiled at him, her equilibrium regained.

He leaned toward her, startling her so much she couldn't move before his lips touched hers, ever so briefly. She flinched and put a hand on his chest, then dropped it back to the desk. "You have a lot of fucking nerve," she said, her voice strong. "Please go."

He grinned, pushed himself away from the desk and stood for a few seconds, his legs wide apart, his shoulders set, hands on his hips as if facing some kind of obstacle to be breached. "I'll go," he declared. "But I'll be back."

Gayle pointed to the closed door. Noah walked backward, never taking his eyes off her. She took a minute to take in his near-perfect body, cover-model face and thick head of dark blond hair, making sure he understood she was ogling him right back. They played the stare-down game for a few more seconds until he made it to the door, opened it, winked at her then ducked out, giving a loud farewell to Susan.

She waited for a few minutes, fingertips pressed against the desk top, jaw tight, teeth grinding. For the first time in a long one her thoughts didn't go directly to Ethan, and her first emotion wasn't fury at him for leaving her, for taking their little boy on that fucking plane.

At the thought of her son, an excruciating pain ripped through her chest, settling in her gut, making her legs wobble. Her boy. She'd lost her boy. A scream bubbled up from her throat, but she tamped it down, dropping into her chair and putting her head down on the cool glass surface in front of her.

Her therapist had been after her for months to say his name, but she'd refused. It was as if accepting Ethan's death by fiery, terrifying plane crash was more than enough. The reality she'd been living with, that she'd scattered two sets of ashes off the balcony of their home before she called the realtor to list it, had been the basic fact she'd been suppressing.

"Liam. Oh God. Liam," she whispered, scrabbling around in her purse for something and muttering her son's name over and over under her breath. After a few desperate seconds, she turned the damn thing upside down and sent the contents rolling across her desk. Finally, she found what she'd been looking for and held it in both hands, staring down at the last photo she'd been able to find of them all together. It had been floating around in the bag for months, purposefully ignored by her, but left there, just in case she needed it.

She stared down into his face, caught in a laughing moment—the kid had always been laughing, so it hadn't been hard to do. She and Ethan had their arms around him and were looking at each other over his head. She remembered the moment now, like it had happened two seconds ago. She recalled exactly what Ethan had said.

"We're lucky," he'd said. "This kid will never not smile for a camera."

She'd said, "Well, he comes by it naturally. You won't ever not smile for a camera, or a pretty lady."

He'd made a fake 'who, me?' face and she'd given him her best 'spare me' look. Liam had kept laughing. The photographer had kept snapping the pictures.

She touched his face—the boy she'd wanted so desperately she'd endured miscarriages, the hormone shots turning her into a weepy, sloppy mess, until Ethan had thrown the whole lot of them out the window of their bedroom with a loud shout and a curse. "Fuck this shit, Gayle. I don't care if we have a baby. I don't. I swear I don't." He'd dropped to his knees in front of her as she'd sobbed her way through another evening, wrapped his arms around her legs and pressed his face into her lap. "I can't stand this anymore. I can't bear to see you this unhappy. Let's enjoy our lives and stop worrying about babies."

She'd conceived Liam that night and he'd been born three weeks early, yet perfectly healthy. She'd never been happier in her life. Ethan had been beyond ecstatic, staying home with her and curling up beside her while she nursed or napped. It had been yet another extension of the extreme fairy tale she'd managed to conjure for herself somehow. Gayle put the picture down on the desk and stared at it, willing herself to accept the totality of her loss.

Interestingly, the tears seemed to have dried up, even as she released the memories of him, of her baby, her little boy, into her brain and let them spill over, subsuming her memories of her life with Ethan. "Susan," she called out. "What else do I have scheduled today?"

"Not much, really." The woman stood in the doorway, a tablet in her hands. "Are you all right?"

"No, I'm not. I need to go home."

Susan nodded and poked at her tablet's screen. "I'll take care of it. You go on. Get some rest."

"Yes. Rest." Gayle picked up the photo and gazed around at the mess she'd made from her purse. "Rest."

Susan poked her head back in the office after a few minutes, startling Gayle out of her semi-trance. "I've canceled and rescheduled everything. Do you need some help?" Susan stood by the desk and stared down at the detritus of pens, lipsticks, tampons, paper clips, credit card receipts, old mints.

"No. I'm fine. Thanks." She started scooping everything back into her bag, leaving the photo on the middle of the glass. She'd spoken more sharply than she'd meant to. "I'm sorry, Susan. I don't mean to…"

But the sympathetic look she'd gotten used to was back. She blew out a breath and got up, leaving the photo where it was and shouldering her purse. "Let Ben know I'll be in tomorrow as usual, but I need some t-t-t-t-time." She shocked herself with her inability to speak. "Thanks."

"No problem," the woman said. She looked down at the photo, then up at Gayle, her face a mask of sadness. "Oh, honey. I'm so—"

Gayle held up a hand. "I know. You're sorry." She grabbed the picture and jammed it back into her purse. "I'll, um, see you tomorrow." She ducked her head and fast-walked out into the hall, past a few clumps of people still hanging around after the meeting and straight to the elevator. When it took forever to arrive, she whirled and headed for the stairwell, ignoring all the stares of everyone around her whose lives were normal, who lived every day with their loved ones and never gave a single thought to what they'd do if it were all yanked away from them in an eye blink. Like she'd done, until the eye blink had happened and she'd been left a hollow shell, a sorry excuse for a woman — a childless widow who cried at the slightest provocation.

"Fuck sorry."

She smiled at the memory of Noah's words, and wondered how many times she'd say 'no' before she said 'yes' to his invitation for a 'chat'.

Chapter Eleven

"You're crazy, little brother. Certifiable. I don't care how hot she is, if she's got that much baggage, you're setting yourself up for disappointment, if not full-on trauma."

Noah rolled his eyes at his reflection in the mirror, waiting for his sister to finish her harangue. "Noah? Are you even listening to me?"

"Yes, ma'am," he lied, looking for a pair of suitable shorts and a T-shirt. "But I have to go now. Time for my first hot yoga class."

Her sigh hit his ears like a tornado—so loud he held the phone away from his ear. "God, you really are serious."

"Yes. I really am serious about my fitness." He flexed one arm, admired his guns for a few seconds and wondered how in the world he'd keep from falling asleep in some silly stretching class. The two weeks between that oddly poignant moment in Gayle's office and today had been busy, with him learning his new job, glad-handing, pouring or buying beers for bar owners and patrons, getting earfuls about quality from some and glowing reviews from others. He'd enjoyed it, but the low-lying memories of her vulnerability in front of him wouldn't ever fully exit his consciousness.

He'd embarked on a bit of subterfuge. After memorizing the hot yoga studio's schedule he'd discovered she wasn't terribly reliable when it came to the time of day she'd participate. Luckily, his job allowed for a fair bit of 'in between' time—normally dead periods when he'd be between retailer calls. So, he spent those hours staking out the place, watching to see when she was there for a class and when she wasn't.

And now, he was ready to make his move. Or rather, ready to give the yoga thing a shot, during a ten a.m. Saturday class he'd discovered, through his amateur sleuthing, that she nearly always attended.

"Noah," his sister barked in his ear. "Don't get caught up in this. She sounds like she might not be worth the emotional effort. How old is she anyway? What if she can't have kids?"

"Sister dear, do you have any idea how crazy you sound right now? I mean, in one breath you're telling me to avoid her, the next you're wondering about nieces and nephews." He made a tsk-ing sound with his teeth. "I mean, really. Make up your mind already."

"Way to deflect me, jerk. Nicely done."

"Thank you. It's but one of my many skills."

"Yeah, yeah. Fuck you anyway."

"No thanks. Tell Rob and the spawn I said hi. I gotta go now. Time for yoga." He hung up before she could berate him any further. He'd read he should bring a yoga mat, a towel to cover it and a water bottle. He'd bought the first and gathered the rest and, with only a mild shiver of anxiety about how she might react at the sight of him invading her space again, he got into his truck and headed for the studio.

He spotted her walking in the door as he parked so he waited a few minutes, hoping she'd have time to get away from the front desk while he paid and signed up or whatever he had to do. Once he'd registered and been given the basics—no talking, wait for first scheduled water break, stay in the room if possible—he left his shoes on one of the open shelves and headed into to the darkened room.

The smell hit him first. His impression was one of a car full of hockey gear, left in the desert for a week. Noticing that none of the people already in the room were gagging or otherwise acknowledging the reek, he stumbled to an empty spot, unrolled his mat and arranged the towel on top it. At a loss for how to manage to not puke, he sat, not even noting where Gayle was located.

With only five minutes before the official class start time, he observed most people were lying down with their feet to the back wall, arms to their sides, breathing quietly. The heat made its presence known once his olfactory nerves adjusted. He could hear motors running somewhere above him and realized with some alarm the light sheen of sweat already coating his arms.

Determined not to panic, or even worry too much— yoga was only a bunch of stretching after all, hot room or no—he closed his eyes and focused on something else that didn't reek of old socks or make him feel like he'd walked into a steam room on a hot summer day. This couldn't be hard, for crying out loud. He was in tip-top shape. He could run ten miles, take a few breaths and run ten more. He could bench press twice his body weight and do hundreds of sit-ups in a row. Noah opened his eyes when the lights came on, flooding the space and prodding everyone to their feet.

He followed their lead, casting a quick glance around the crowded room. He didn't see her right away, since he'd had to tuck himself into a corner and was surrounded by mostly women in various stages of nakedness. He blinked, attempting to parse the amount of bare female flesh, some of it covered in sports bras and spandex.

The teacher lady was, in a word, hot. Okay, a few more — AF. He gulped and looked down at his feet, the heat filling his lungs and nasal passages while she made word noises he barely registered.

My God, I'm dripping with sweat already. How in the hell am I going to get through this?

When he realized everyone around him was shifting and assuming some kind of preparatory position, he copied them. When he looked toward the instructor chick, he looked right into her eyes and realized she remembered him. Her brow furrowed as she snuck a glance to her left, then glared back at him. He smiled, or at least he tried to. It might have not looked much like it. His brain felt as if it were melting into a warm puddle of goo. The teacher grinned at him, cleared her throat and the class began.

At first, it was only breathing. But it seemed to go on forever. And the realization he was sucking in huge lungs full of the stinking, overheated air made him dizzy. He tried his level best to follow along, to do what the others were doing. After the third, or perhaps the fourth, borderline torturous position he was asked to fold himself into, he reached for his water bottle, gasping, every inch of his skin drenched.

"Please hold off on a water break for one more posture," the teacher bitch's voice boomed into the room. He put the water bottle down.

The entire experience seemed designed to bring him to his knees, while everyone around him flexed and stretched and generally prezteled themselves with seemingly little effort. Everyone was dripping wet by the time they hit the floor, finally. But there were still forty minutes to go. He tried to obey the torturer-woman's commands to breathe through his nose to calm his heartbeat but lying on his belly for some set of 'spine-strengthening series' made him gasp like a beached fish.

At one point, he realized he'd poured the last of the water into his mouth and could only sit and stare down at the wet towel beneath him as he attempted not to run out of the room — or throw up his guts. This had been the single most hare-brained idea of his stupid, woman-chasing life. He couldn't wait to get the fuck out and never, ever come back.

"Now, please, lie back and let your body absorb the amazing experience you've just given it," the woman trilled. Noah flopped onto his back. In all his years of working out — running, biking, lifting and swimming — he'd never once felt like this. It was the typical wet-noodle sensation he'd achieve after a hard two hours or so working up a sweat, but this was combined with a kind of hollowed-out, drained feeling that made him close his eyes and drift, even though he was still lying in this disgusting-smelling hot space.

When he finally opened his eyes, he realized someone was crouched over him. He flinched and propped on his elbows, embarrassed by the state of his skin and the stink emanating from his every pore.

"You didn't do too badly," Gayle said, holding out her hand. He frowned but took it and let her tug him forward and up to his feet. The room was dark and empty, but for the two of them.

"Shit," he said, reaching for his water bottle before remembering its empty state. "I didn't think I'd fall asleep."

"It's more relaxing than you think – I mean, when you're doing it."

Noah couldn't resist the grin. She frowned at him, dark strands of her hair in sweaty curls around her flushed face. He raised an eyebrow and shrugged. "Sorry. Can't sweat the letch out of me, I guess." Realizing he'd probably blown it again, he reached down to roll his dripping towel up in the yoga mat. When he rose, Gayle hadn't moved. But she was smiling – a kind of half-smile, both wistful and hopeful. He decided maybe this had been a good idea after all, sweat, stink and near-death experience included.

He was about to ask her to join him for coffee, or a shot of something healthy, like kale juice, when she turned away and walked out of the room, sending a glorious puff of cool air across his body. He shivered and followed her, sheepish when he realized everyone had been watching them but were now busily pretending they hadn't been.

His flesh prickled into goosebumps and he tugged his sweatshirt down his bare torso. The effort made him almost topple over, so he dropped onto his butt on the bench and propped his elbows on his knees, trying to regain his equilibrium. A few deep breaths later, he thought he might live. But there was no way he was going to walk out of here just yet. He lunged forward and refilled his water bottle, gulping it down so fast it leaked out of the sides of his mouth. As he went for a second refill, a hand touched his shoulder, making him flinch and send water flying across the sealed concrete floor.

He was shaking now, having some kind of DT freak-out. He circled right back around to this-was-a-stupid-idea-land. "Jesus." He ran a hand down his face and watched the teacher drop a fresh towel on his spillage and calmly mop it up. As he stood, staring like a dumb-ass, Gayle emerged from the ladies' locker room, her hair up in a towel, her skin red and shining, her body covered in a batik-blue sundress that made his poor, overworked heart stutter in his chest.

He smiled, then stepped back from her, hyper-aware of how much he reeked, but unwilling to let this opportunity pass. "Hey, uh, so could we…could I buy you… I mean…"

She leaned her head to one side, the smile he wanted to kiss so badly ghosting across her lips. He put his hands on his hips, looked down, took a breath then stared into her eyes. He was usually better at this. But she'd turned him into a rattled, stuttering, teenager-like mess. The teacher was standing next to Gayle now, her dark eyes narrow when she glared at him. He nodded in her direction. "Interesting stuff in there. Thanks. I think."

She crossed her arms. "You're pretty stiff, but I can tell you're in good shape." Her gaze darted down his front then back up again. He blushed hot, her double entendre settling into his psyche. These women were messing with him. He stood straighter, part of him wanting to prove to them both—but mostly to Gayle— he wasn't here to stalk her or anything more than to get to know her. But it sure as hell wasn't what it looked like and he knew it.

He held up both hands. "Okay, all right, ladies. I get it. I'm at your mercy." He used his best seducer-smoky gaze on the teacher. She took a step away. Satisfied he'd set her back at least a half second, he turned his attention to Gayle. She was studying him like a specimen under a microscope. He cleared his throat. "Could I buy you something super healthy to drink, after I've had a shower?"

Her beautiful smile widened, which made his entire body clench in anticipation. Dear Jesus, but she was perfection, despite what he knew about her backstory. It wasn't like his was anything to write home about. And all he wanted was to sit, drink something gross but good for him and talk to her.

"Tell you what," she said, after smiling at her friend the teacher. "You come back tomorrow and get through another class, and I'll think about it."

He gaped at her. "Tomorrow? Hell no. I'll need a week to recover from this shit."

"Actually, the more classes you can string together, the better."

"Fuck. That. No offense."

"None taken." The teacher put a hand on Gayle's arm. "I'll leave him to you." Her dark eyes flashed when she looked at him. "I think you can handle it." He wasn't quite sure whom she meant but it didn't matter.

"So, about that kale juice…"

She chuckled and walked past him, brushing his arm with hers. He ground his teeth, dying to reach for her but stuck in his cloud of stink, and, frankly, mortification at how amateurish he sounded. "I told you. Come back tomorrow. Then I'll consider it."

He stared straight ahead, not willing to give her the satisfaction of staring at her ass as she left him there.

When he showed up the next day, more prepared for the sensory onslaught, she wasn't in the yoga room. By the time the instructor flipped on the lights, she'd still not shown. Noah stood, met the teacher's steady gaze for a few seconds then focused on himself for the next unbearable ninety minutes and left the studio without a word to anyone. Gayle, it seemed, had decided to give the hot room a skip.

Chapter Twelve

Gayle sat, staring at her computer screen without seeing it, her coffee long gone cold in the cup at her elbow. Her mind refused to settle, to let her focus on the work in front of her. With a curse, she pushed her chair back from the glass-topped desk, swiveling her chair so she faced the floor-to-ceiling window. The view — of the carefully groomed courtyard below being used by a group of warehouse employees for some kind of a celebration — didn't help her state of mind either.

She shouldn't have skipped the damn yoga class last Sunday. It'd been a real bitch move and she knew it. Because she also knew in her soul Noah would show, she'd sat, frozen behind the steering wheel, staring at the door, watching people head in for the class. Then, without understanding why, she'd sped out of the parking lot, gone home and sat in her frilly, teenaged room for hours in silence.

She didn't need this aggravation. She didn't want anything from him. Being the sad widow suited her. It was her life now and she had no reason to change it.

Well, no reason other than the fact of Noah's extreme, handsome, somehow calming attention.

"Crap." She rose and started pacing her office, dragging her fingers through her hair and spending another forty-five minutes ignoring the emails piling up in her inbox. It was that or allow her thoughts of him to turn in a direction which was, without a doubt, erotic and utterly inappropriate in a most breathtaking manner.

When she'd stood there, inches from his sweaty, bare torso, it had taken everything in her not to reach out and swipe her finger down his chest, across his shoulders, up his neck. Hours later, she still hadn't shaken the fact of that effort. Not to mention how half-flirty, half-bitchy she'd been to him about his innocent request to go out and have a chat. She found herself facing the blank wall, graced by innocuous framed photos of random Michigan scenes, once again not seeing anything but a line of sweat trickling down the young man's neck.

"Hey, Gayle?"

The sound of the voice behind her, intruding on her mental battle not to imagine Noah's young, strong, naked body alongside her somewhat less young, but newly strong one, made her jump away from the wall and turn to face her assistant. "Yes. What? Sorry." She ran her hand down her face, furious at her weakness, her non-thinking about her dead husband and son. *What's wrong with me?*

The next few hours were spent putting out a fire or two, something she normally despised since it implied a lack of planning on someone's part. Today, she welcomed the distraction of it — making calls to a large grocery chain to calm someone's ruffled feathers, dealing with a riled-up brewery owner, chewing out the printing company that screwed up their latest order of shelf-talkers. It was such a relief to re-locate her focus on this — her job, the one thing that mattered to her now.

At three-thirty she came up for air and realized the reason her stomach hurt was because she'd not eaten since a morning slice of toast. With a sigh, she leaned back in her chair, still clutching her phone where she'd just spent a half-hour reassuring three different brewery owners they were not being dropped from the TriCities portfolio. She closed her burning eyes for a few seconds, letting her mind rest from the fire-fighting efforts. She drifted, taking long, deep breaths in and out through her nose. Part of her realized she was about to doze, even as the already dozing part treated her to another flash memory of Noah — his deep brown eyes, chiseled face and dripping wet torso. The dream filled her mind. She tried to force herself awake, but instead, her subconscious took over, and she let it.

* * * *

"Why did you stand me up?" the dream-Noah asked. His hands rested on his hips and his handsome brow was furrowed with anger. "Kind of a real bitch move, Gayle."

She took a dream step back from him, afraid, and yet wanting to touch him, to lean forward, to go up on her tiptoes and run her eager tongue across his broad shoulder. But the more moves away from him she took in her mind, the closer the man seemed to get. His face filled her vision — full, lush lips, nose that looked like it had been broken at least once and those huge, brown-gold eyes. Gayle's skin prickled in response to his dream-proximity. His nostrils flared. His cheeks flushed even redder. His breathing changed, moving into a faster gear. The wall pressed against her back as he continued to loom over her, not touching her but apparently getting turned on in spite of it all.

His skin was warm — hot — under her hands. The sculpted musculature of his chest, his abs, his shoulders, arms, back and ass felt exactly the way she'd imagined them. She looked down at her fingers, marveling that they stroked, traced, gripped and groped his flesh while he stood and let her do it, immobile other than his chest, which moved faster the busier her hands got.

He was, in a word, perfect. Like some kind of a young, studly god, dropped into her world at a moment when she was only just getting her mind wrapped around her new, Michigan-based reality. He was unreal, but yet completely real under her now trembling hands. She was on some kind of a weird cougar-kick, but heaven help her, she could not stop touching him.

"Kiss me," he whispered. His hands were propped on the wall behind her. He wasn't as tall as her dead husband had been. But with her standing next to him, sweaty skin to skin and barefoot, apparently post-hot dream-yoga, he was tall enough so when she decided to do what he'd asked, she had to go up a bit on her toes to get to his lips. She stared at them, auto-comparing them to Ethan's as they filled her vision.

"Stop," he said, perhaps reading her mind. "I'm not him. I'll never be him. He's not coming back. But I'm here." He kissed her then, this too-handsome young man in her midafternoon office dream. But it was short-lived. When he broke away, leaving her gasping and leaning forward so far she almost fell into him, he gripped her elbows. "Stop it, Gayle. I mean it. Just stop."

"Stop...what?"

"Stop being sad."

Her heart raced as she reached for him, needing his lips on hers, wanting his arms around her so badly she felt tears welling behind her eyes. "I'm a widow. I lost my little boy. I'm supposed to be sad."

But Noah was retreating from her now, taking his near-naked body and firm, full lips with him. "Not anymore," he said, his voice fading. "I don't think you should be sad anymore."

She stopped and crossed her arms, coming just short of stamping her foot on the floor in anger. "You don't get to tell me how to feel."

He'd turned away from her and was fading into the clouds of her dreaming mind, but when she said that, he whirled back around, grabbed her and dragged her close, so close she felt every solid inch of him. But he didn't kiss her again. He just stared into her eyes. "No, I don't get to tell you. I get to show you." He traced his fingertip across her lips, her jaw, down her neck and shoulder, leaving a line of virtual fire on her skin.

"Then fucking show me already," she demanded, threading her fingers into his still-damp hair. His lips— her current point of focus—turned up in a slight, wistful smile. Anger filled her chest. She reached down with her other hand and cupped the erection straining the front of his shorts, smiling when he flinched and closed his eyes. "I can tell you want to show me...something."

As she was leaning forward to press her lips to the sweat on his neck, he broke from her, fading away into the mist of her dream, leaving her hanging, as horny as she'd been in years. "God damn it," she spat into the gathering darkness. "God damn you...God damn you, Ethan." But she'd meant Noah, hadn't she?

The tears — the infernal, eternal tears — spilled down her cheeks when she shivered in the aftermath of dwindling adrenaline. She was still pressed against the wall, its solidity keeping her from falling to the floor. But her body was now wracked with tremors, sobs bursting from her, filling the air around her, and she slid slowly down until her butt hit the floor.

"Gayle, stop," Noah's voice floated out of the mist around her.

"Go to hell," she croaked, wrapping her arms around her bent legs. "Go. To Hell. Leave me alone! I'm fine. I don't need you!"

"Gayle...stop," he repeated.

"Stop...what? Stop bossing me around."

* * * *

"Gayle." A hand landed on her shoulder, another one seemed to cup her elbow and lift her up. "Calm down. It's all right."

Her eyes flew open. The first thing she saw was the acoustic tile ceiling of her office. The next thing was Noah's face. His golden-brown eyes were full of concern. His lips — dear Lord and sonny Jesus help her, those lips — were pressed together. She saw another face—Susan's, her assistant's. It was also creased with worry. She blinked fast, confused by the fact that she seemed to be lying on the floor.

Mortified, she rose up on her elbows, noting her desk chair now lying on its side nearby. "Stop," Noah said, making her shiver all over at the dream memory of him saying those words to her as she tried to sit, to stand, to regain the tattered remnants of her dignity.

Susan handed her a bottle of water. "Here. Drink this."

She brushed a strand of her hair out of her face and took the bottle, relishing the sensation of his warm hand propping her up, even though she despised the way he'd seemed to appear from her dream, albeit wearing more clothing, to observe her latest embarrassing scene. She downed the water fast, surprised at how thirsty she was. Swiping at the trickles escaping down her chin, she frowned at him. But he didn't move. He just sat, watching her with a concerned yet neutral expression on his face.

"Okay. I'm fine now." She held out her arm. He took it and eased her to her feet.

"How long since you've eaten anything?" He hadn't let go of her arm yet and still had his palm planted in the small of her back. Gayle wanted to move out of his reach. But she didn't. If anything, she leaned into him slightly, her mind still lodged in a pleasant dream-state.

"This morning. Jesus, what time is it, anyway?"

"Almost five-thirty," Susan said from somewhere in the room. The sound of her assistant's voice brought Gayle crashing back into reality. She pulled away from Noah's warm grip, ran her hands down her now-wrinkly skirt and shirt front and lifted her chin. Susan was scurrying around, righting the chair, straightening papers on her desk, irritating the crap out of her. But she understood the woman's desire to do something, anything, to put what had just happened into some kind of perspective.

"The perfect time to call it quits and get an early dinner," he declared, not taking his gaze from her face.

"Maybe for you," she said, her voice sharp — too sharp — but she had to get control of this situation. And the only way that would happen was if Noah got the hell out of her space. He needed to get the hell out of her life, before she made a complete fool out of herself.

"Nope, not just for me." He grabbed her phone from the floor, where it must have landed when she fell off her chair in the grips of a near wet dream. She glared at him, but he kept his face calm, reaching over to shut her laptop and pluck her purse from the floor where it had slipped off the back of the chair. He tucked the phone into the bag and held it out to her, his grin wide and sincere and so perfect she could barely repress a shudder of desire.

Instead, she snatched her purse from him, jammed it up on her shoulder and headed for the door. But he beat her to it somehow, opening it and putting his hand on her back again. She moved forward, perhaps to put herself out of his reach. He moved with her, staying close, too close, and they made their way to the metal staircase.

Thankfully, the lower office areas were mostly deserted — typical for a Friday evening. Gayle tried not to envision what the few remaining employees saw when they looked up to see who was descending from the executive office level. But she knew they were taking it all in — their new sales director, the woman with the tragic backstory, walking way too close to a man way too young for her to be daydreaming about.

She stiffened as they walked through the wide space between the stairs and the front door. When they hit the oppressive heat of the summer evening, she jerked herself away from him and walked toward away, determined to escape and go home alone to nurse her ego. But once again, he beat her to her car and stood leaning against her driver's-side door, beaming at her. She rolled her eyes.

"Move. Please." She crossed her arms. Her legs were shaking with the wave of dizziness which hit her, but she bit the inside of her cheek to hide it from him.

He held out his hand. She stared at it — it was huge, like an overgrown puppy's paw. The familiar anger rolled up from her chest, burning her throat on its way to her brain. "Stop treating me like...like..." She sighed, finding herself fading again. Would there ever be a time when she didn't do something stupid or embarrassing in front of this man? Her vision seemed to go gray from the outside in. The heat rose from the dark asphalt beneath her feet.

Noah grabbed her arm, hustled her around to the passenger side of her own damn car and tucked her into the seat. Exhaustion made her floppy and slow-witted as she watched him jog back around to the driver's side, then climb in behind the steering wheel. His huge, boyish grin made a fresh bolt of white-hot lust shoot down her spine, settling low in her stomach, and still lower. She pressed her thighs together and balled her hands into fists, determined to ignore this — to ignore him — so she could get back to what remained of her life.

"Where to?" he asked, going for the ignition button. The powerful engine roared to life. She glared straight ahead, demanding that her mind not go into its usual comparison mode. Ethan had been one of those men who always insisted on driving, which had rubbed her the wrong way at first, since she was one of those women who preferred to drive herself.

"Just take me home," she said, her voice cracking with stress.

"I think we should go somewhere else — somewhere we can eat and talk."

She sighed, pressed her still-balled fists against the dash in front of her. "Fine. You decide. I don't care."

He screeched into the heavy rush-hour traffic and navigated the roads expertly without a word. When he pulled up in front of a familiar, old building with a small, faded sign, she shot him a surprised glance. "How do you know about this place?"

He chuckled, released his belt and turned to look at her. She averted her gaze, unable to take it. "Are you kidding me? My brother-in-law owns this dive."

She opened her mouth to respond, but he'd climbed out and was standing at her door, holding out a hand to help her. She put hers into it, recognizing and owning the way her skin responded to their contact. For a split second they stood together, close enough to kiss, inside the open car door. But he moved away, blinking fast, so she could get all the way out and shut the door behind her. He held out a hand. "After you," he said, his eyes shining. "Hope you like a greasy burger."

"I can't imagine anything better," she admitted, her mouth already watering at the smell. Noah had his hand in the small of her back again, guiding her through the door into the dim space that still held a mild aura of old cigarette smoke. It was so comforting, so perfect.

And so wrong.

He guided her to a table, held out her chair, put a hand on her shoulder and waved to the bleached blonde behind the bar.

"Hey, honey," she called out, her grin wide. "What'cha drinkin'?"

"Bring us a couple of Fitzgerald ambers," he said, reaching up to catch the kiss she blew in his direction. "Thanks, doll."

"Wow. Sexist much?" Gayle said when he sat across from her. She realized she was gripping her purse in front of her like some old lady in church.

"Huh?" He smiled at her, but waved at a few other people, and spent a few minutes calling out greetings. When the woman brought their beers—poured perfectly, Gayle noted, a half inch of foamy head above a lovely red brew dancing with carbonation—Noah patted her ass. The woman patted his head in response and pulled out a pad of paper.

"The usual for you, darlin'?"

He sipped, nodded then pointed across the table. "Make it two," he said.

The woman looked at Gayle, narrowed her eyes then frowned at the young man, who'd managed to down half his beer. "She looks like a chef salad type to me. You sure?"

"Um, I'm right here," Gayle said, her female-competition hackles rising so high she figured they were visible to the entire room. "And if his 'usual' includes a giant, medium rare burger with orange cheese, a slice of tomato and onion with a side of fries, then that is definitely more my type. Thanks." She sipped her beer.

Noah grinned over at her, then up at the still-frowning woman. "What can I say? She's a mind reader."

"All right then." She jotted something on her pad, shot Gayle a look that would literally have killed her, if it contained a single dagger, then sashayed back to the bar. Noah watched her go. He finished his beer, then turned back to face Gayle, his grin still wide and mischievous.

"You're a pig," she declared, before staring down at the remains of her own beer. "Jesus, this is good."

"Yep. It is. It's our best seller right now." He held up two fingers toward the bar. Gayle ignored the ugly glare the woman treated her to and focused on the man across from her. "What?" he asked, holding out his arms. "You're gonna fault me for treating her the way she wants?"

"How do you know that's what she wants?"

"Tricia's been working here for almost twenty-five years. She's the bar manager, the overlord, the mama bear. And she likes for men to let her know she's pretty."

Gayle glanced over at the woman, who was pouring beers and chattering with the gathering crowd. She was fifty if she was a day. And she'd definitely been pretty, once. Now she seemed to be a strong, capable, woman in charge. As if sensing her stare, Tricia looked right at Gayle, glanced over at Noah, winked then treated Gayle to more angry glaring.

"She's a little overprotective," he admitted. "She knows I'm prone to make shitty choices and likes to remind me of them."

Their beers appeared, brought this time by a young waitress. Noah treated her to his most sincere smile. "Thanks, Dana. How's your mom doing?"

"Better, thanks for asking." She blushed to the roots of her hair. Gayle watched them exchange a few more words, Noah using a kind, respectful, completely different voice with the obviously flustered young woman than he'd used with the brassy Tricia.

"Oh, you are good," she said, once Dana had made her reluctant way over to a different table.

Noah raised a dark eyebrow, sipped, then set the beer down and leaned forward on his elbows. "I am, yes," he admitted, in a tone that made her scalp tingle. "But maybe not for the reasons you think." He shrugged, leaned back in his chair and seemed suddenly vulnerable. Gayle frowned and looked away, berating herself for getting caught up in his weird, female-enticing game.

"Thank you," she said, keeping her hand wrapped around the cold beer glass.

"For what?" He kept his casual stance, but his gaze was fixed on her in a way that made her feel as if she were the only female in his universe.

Stop it, Gayle. Don't be ridiculous. The man is a nonstop flirt machine and you've just watched him work.

She held up her glass. He touched his to it. They sipped and set them down, still staring at each other. "For being here for me." She meant it. It was way more complicated, of course, but right then, she couldn't think of any other way to say it. To her surprise, Noah stretched out his arm and held his hand out, palm up, on the table in front of her. She blinked down at it, unwilling to see it for what it was. If she put her hand in his, it would be a sign, a line crossed, a Rubicon breached, the divide between her life as a miserable, barely functioning, childless widow and her new one filled with possibility. Filled with him.

She squeezed her eyes shut, willing him to withdraw the gesture. When she opened them, he had both his hands out, palms up in front of her. His eyes were soft and kind, nonthreatening and expectant of nothing. In a slight daze, she put her hands into his. He closed his fingers around them, warming her instantly.

"What is this?" she whispered, her lips trembling. "I don't understand it."

"Don't try," he insisted, still gripping her, anchoring her to earth. "Just enjoy it."

He lifted her left hand to his lips and kissed the knuckle of her ring finger softly, then let go of her when their huge plates of cardiac-event-inducing food arrived. She stared at him through the rising heat. He smiled, picked up his burger and took an enormous bite. Her stomach clenched and her mouth watered when she looked down at her food. When she picked up the enormous burger and bit into it, she couldn't resist a groan of pure satisfaction.

As she wiped the grease off her lips and chin, she saw Noah was frozen, his half-eaten burger still in his hand. He blinked, then his perfect lips parted in a smile that was not sweet—not in the slightest. But it was no less compelling. "I like the noise you made," he said, leaning over the table. He touched his fingertip to the corner of her lips and drew away with a blot of mustard on it. "I could get used to it." He stuck his finger in his mouth.

"Cheesy," she declared, taking another giant bite and sighing with pleasure when the perfectly disgusting

Liz Crowe

combination of half-rare ground beef, tart tomato, crisp onion and hot mustard rolled across her tongue.

"Maybe," he agreed, before taking his own bite and turning the whole process into some kind of a seduction scene worthy of the most purple-prose-riddled romance novel. "But it's true."

"Shut up already," she said. "Let me concentrate on this meal."

"Sure thing," he said with a somewhat less lascivious grin. "Let's drink to it." He held up his glass. She clinked hers and sipped.

"What did I just drink to?" She dredged some of the steak fries through a puddle of ketchup.

"To the sound you make when you're happy. The one I'm going to enjoy hearing you make. A lot."

She rolled her eyes at him. But her body was sending a far different signal. One she was going to have a hell of a hard time resisting.

"This isn't a date, just to make it clear." She ate a few more fries, sipped her beer and enjoyed the comfortable silence in the wake of that statement.

"Well, actually, Gayle, it is."

She frowned, watching him demolish the rest of his burger then start on his fries.

"I mean, you can pretend all you want. But you know as well as I do what this is."

For a lack of any coherent response, she plowed into her own food, enjoying every last decadent bite of it. She couldn't recall the last time she'd had what Ethan used to call 'a slutty cheeseburger', so she determined to enjoy the experience, and the company, even with her mind yammering at her that this whole thing was weird, wrong, strange, all of the above.

Chapter Thirteen

Gayle sliced lemons into a big glass of water, sprinkled in some sea salt then handed the thing over to Evelyn. Her friend took it and tried a few sips before setting it down and leaning back on her couch with a wince.

"Good Christ, somebody just kill me. This is the worst feeling ever."

"You didn't get sick with Rose?"

"Not this bad, and not this early, either. Ugh."

Gayle patted Evelyn's knee, picked up the glass and made her take a few more sips. They were supposed to be going out to get their nails done then have dinner. When she'd arrived at Evelyn's house, she'd discovered the poor woman crouched in the bathroom, shivering and puking while Austin had looked on helplessly with Rose tugging at his pants leg and demanding to know why Mommy was sick.

Gayle had jumped right in, telling Austin to take Rose outside to the pool for an evening dip to distract her while she dealt with Evelyn. She'd cleaned up the bathroom while her friend had showered, then called for pizza before making what Ethan's mother had insisted she drink during her days of pregnancy misery. It had worked, at least for a few hours at a time, but it took some getting used to—the sour saltiness had seemed an anathema at first, but she'd gotten to where she craved it through the early months.

After she'd managed to choke the whole glass down, Evelyn admitted to feeling a smidgeon above suicidal, and went downstairs to choose a wine for Gayle and Austin to share. As she sat flipping through a beverage industry magazine, Gayle's phone buzzed with yet another text. Knowing who it was from, she ignored it as long as she could manage before tugging her phone from her jeans pocket and staring down at Noah's latest missive. In the five weeks since she'd fallen out of her office chair and been treated to a slutty cheeseburger and not-too-subtle flirting, she and Noah had eased into something approximating a relationship that she kept firmly on a friends-only level, complete with three-days-a-week hot yoga followed by green smoothies or, if they were feeling decadent, ice cream.

He'd asked every weekend to be granted the honor of her company on a real date—dinner, dancing, movie, orchestra concert, nightclubbing, poetry reading, whatever she wanted. But she'd held him off, concocting a wide array of excuses to keep him at arm's length. Every time she'd convinced herself it was the right thing to do. That no matter how much more she got to know about him—his honesty about his past, his frustration about his future, his wicked sense of humor, and most importantly his deep desire to get to know her better—she didn't want any more.

She didn't deserve any more. She was a sad, broken widow and determined to stay that way. There was no room in her world for someone like him — a…a…plaything, a boy toy. But he was more, and she damn well knew it.

She'd caught herself reaching out to him with regular text messages, sharing things about her day, a joke, a frustration, a sad moment. For the last three days, she'd actually forced herself not to do it at all, which had prompted him to be amused by her silence, then aggravated, then a little panicked. Hence, this message.

If you'll just let me know you're ok I swear I'll leave you alone.

Followed quickly by —

Well, I might not leave you alone *alone, if you know what I mean.* (winky face)

Then —

You're fucking w/me aren't u?

And a final one —

You know what? Fine. Leave me to worry.

She stared at the string of messages, her pulse racing at each increasingly intense line. After tapping out and deleting five potential responses, she got up and headed outside. Evelyn emerged from the house, two glasses of wine and one of lemon-choked water on a tray. They sat in silence, watching Austin and Rose cavort around in the pool, and Gayle slowly relaxed.

"So, what's all this I hear about you and my new brand ambassador—the delectable Noah Stokes?"

The sip of wine Gayle had been indulging morphed into a gulp and shot down her windpipe. Evelyn leaned over and pounded her between the shoulder blades until she was able to breathe again. But even then, with her eyes streaming and her face burning hot, she refused to meet her friend's curious gaze. "I don't know what you mean," she finally managed, taking the bottle of water Evelyn handed her.

"Don't bullshit me, my friend." Evelyn smiled at her and patted her knee. "I say go for it. I remember him from Nexus. He's pretty damn hard to forget, isn't he?" She raised an eyebrow and sipped her doctored water, wincing as she swallowed. "God, this is so gross." She flipped a switch near the door. The late-summer evening was hot, but the humidity gripping the area for the last few weeks had broken the night before thanks to a loud, showy thunderstorm that had kept Gayle awake—or rather had given her an excuse to sit and obsess over Noah. The ceiling fan above them on the enclosed porch whipped strands of their hair around their faces. Gayle stared at her friend, her throat frozen with a combination of embarrassment and a need to spill the whole damn thing.

"I...um...I'm...I don't... Shit."

Evelyn sipped her lemon water, waiting Gayle out. As they always managed to do, tears burned her eyes. She clenched her jaw, willing herself not to scream, to cry, to curse, yell, throw things. She'd never in her life felt more conflicted. Even when Ethan had continued to pursue her after their first, steamy, near accidental encounter, she'd never experienced this torn-in-two sensation in her chest and guts. It had been like a cat-and-mouse game with Ethan. This…this was more like a dance—a two-steps-forward, five-steps-back thing leaving her breathless, giddy, ashamed and somehow even more needy.

She hated it. And yet, these last three days she'd gone incommunicado had been beyond unbearable. She loved talking to him, listening to him, laughing at his jokes, tossing his increasingly overt raunchiness right back at him. She missed him. And for that, she hated herself more than ever.

She sipped her wine. Evelyn left her to her thoughts. "I don't deserve…this," Gayle said, more to herself than anyone. "I don't. I don't." She set her glass down before she shattered it between her fingers. Suddenly horrified, she yanked her phone back out and stared down at the date until her vision blurred. She wiped away the single tear that landed on the device's screen, stood and headed inside.

"Mommy! Come in the water with us!" Rose's high, childish voice hit Gayle right between the eyes. "Come on, Mommy! Daddy's getting all prune-y and wants to get out!"

"Later, baby. Mommy needs to talk to Miss Gayle a little longer."

Gayle felt an arm around her shoulders, but she knew she was fading. She'd never been able to look at Rose—at any children her age. She'd even managed to shut out their voices most of the time. But now, the little girl's voice pierced her soul.

"I have to go," she choked out, stumbling over the step up into the kitchen from the deck. She couldn't see. She couldn't hear. She could barely even breathe. She had to get in her car, roll down all the windows and drive as fast as she could — somewhere. Perhaps simply into the nearest oncoming truck. Or better yet, a brick wall.

Here it was again. The day her longed-for son and beloved husband had died in a no-doubt terrifying fireball crash into some fucking corn field in that goddamned private jet. The day she had begun this odd journey from privileged and ecstatic to lonely despair. The day she'd wished she'd been on the stupid plane too, so she didn't have to be left behind, pretending she was all right when she'd never be all right again.

"Gayle, wait," Evelyn called behind her, but Gayle didn't slow her race across their front lawn to her car. *How in God's name could I have let this happen? I...forgot about it? About them? No. Never.*

She jumped into the car's oven-like interior and touched the ignition button. But nothing happened. She tried again, her swampy mind retrieving the fact that she'd left her keys in her purse on Evelyn's coffee table. She had both hands wrapped tight around the steering wheel, figuring she could simply sit in here and asphyxiate herself, die of heat stroke and thirst.

Austin appeared with her keys, hit the Unlock, and Evelyn crouched beside her, brushing sweaty stands of hair off her face. "Gayle, honey, it's all right. You haven't done anything wrong."

She glared at her friend, baring her teeth like some kind of feral animal. "You don't know anything about this, so leave me alone." She sensed rather than saw Austin pulling Evelyn to her feet and taking her place.

"Gayle," he said, his low growl of a voice making her want to scream. "Come back inside. Calm down a few minutes, then I can drive you home if you want."

"Leave. Me. Alone." She stared straight ahead, terrified that if she looked at her friends she'd give in, let them lure her back into their giant, comfortable house with their sweet little girl and their wine cellar and their in-ground pool—all the shit she'd once had. And hers had been much nicer, since her house had overlooked the Pacific Ocean.

Austin Fitzgerald was a rich trust fund kid who'd jumped into the craft beer scene early enough to be super successful and was still making money at it. Ethan Connolly's wealth made Austin's look like a piggy bank on the dresser. Gayle closed her eyes and pressed her forehead into her hands as Ethan's handsome, lined face swam into her consciousness and stuck there, smiling, his thick, graying hair messy, like he'd just gotten out of bed. His blue eyes shone in a familiar, lusty way—the way she'd given in to once, then again and again. And finally, had admitted she loved.

"Oh God," she said, tears finally bursting out of her, coating her cheeks and her hands, and her lap.

She let Evelyn pull her out of the car. Let Austin half carry her back up to the house. Let them both settle her on the couch with her wine and some expensive-looking cheese and bread. Noticed they made a point to keep Rose well clear of her, shushing the little girl and promising her a movie in her room with Daddy.

She sipped her wine and forced her mind to go blank. When Evelyn re-emerged, bringing the pizza which had materialized at some point during her freak-out, she attempted a smile. "I've turned into that woman, haven't I?" She sighed and put her feet on the leather ottoman, finishing off her wine before holding it up for a refill.

"What woman?" Evelyn ignored the pizza, choosing her lemon water instead. Gayle tried hard not to yell at the massive unfairness of this, of her entire life, of where she found herself right now.

"The one everyone tiptoes around, trying not to set off on one of her silly fits." She stared down at her recharged glass. "I'm sorry." She sipped, shocked she could even swallow anything. "I'm really sorry."

"Honey, you don't have a damn thing to be sorry about." Evelyn sat next to her and slipped her arm around Gayle's shoulder. "You're right. I don't know anything about what you're feeling right now but please know I love you and I want to be here for you. Okay?"

Gayle nodded and pressed her face into Evelyn's shoulder, shedding a few more of her endless supply of tears before sitting up and sniffling, surprisingly hungry. The last two years' worth of this particular gruesome anniversary she'd gone almost a week without eating, unable to contemplate doing something so innocuous—simply because Ethan and Liam no longer could do it with her. Guilt slammed into her, making her drop the pizza slice back into the box and slap her hand over her lips to hold back the scream.

Chapter Fourteen

When the doorbell rang, Evelyn jumped up as if she'd been expecting someone. Gayle sniffled and sipped and stared at the food she wanted but couldn't bring herself to enjoy. Muttered voices from the foyer barely made an impression on her so, when she lifted her gaze from the pizza and saw who stood next to Evelyn, she flinched, spilling wine down her hand and wrist to the Turkish rug under her feet. "Shit. I'm sorry." She glared at her friend. "Why is *he* here?"

"He reached out to me earlier today, to make sure you were accounted for, that you had someone to be with, since you weren't answering his texts." Evelyn shrugged, looked from Gayle to Noah and mumbled something about checking on Rose before heading up the back staircase. Noah sat in the chair to her right, elbows on his jeans-clad knees, staring at her. She sighed and looked at the ceiling, then back at him.

"I want…" she began, biting her lip hard, tasting blood with the effort to not finish the sentence. Noah leaned closer to her, took her hand and pressed it to his lips before putting it alongside his clean-shaven cheek. He smiled, tilted his head slightly, keeping her hand under his. They sat like this for several minutes, Gayle's pounding heartbeat slowly calming.

"We should clean this up," he said, letting go of her and heading into the kitchen. When he appeared with a damp cloth and some cleaning solution, she nodded and took her wine glass to the sink while he did some damage control to the rug. She stood watching him, unable to tear her eyes off his ass, until he finished and took everything back into the kitchen.

She followed him, her heart calm, her mind made up, every inch of her skin prickling in anticipation. She waited while he tucked the cleaner away, rinsed the rag and hung it on the empty dish rack. When he turned, she saw something in his eyes that gave her pause on her current trajectory. Something she'd never seen in their gold-brown depths—something that made her believe he truly was the nice guy he claimed to be.

He looked scared.

She took a step closer to him so they were only separated by six inches of highly charged air. Putting her hand over his heart, she smiled when it raced under her palm. "I want you to take me home and make love to me, Noah Stokes."

He blinked a few times. His heart beat even faster. He shook his head and backed away, stopping when his butt hit the granite-topped island. His eyes darkened and his face flushed, but he kept shaking his head as she approached him and put both her hands alongside his cheeks. "I want this. I need this. I'm ready…"

"You don't and you aren't," he declared, taking her hands off his face. Fury roiling up in her, she yanked him closer, went up on her toes and kissed him, hard, shoving her tongue between his lips, relishing the taste of him, the sensation of his strong, hard body pressed against hers.

He resisted for about a quarter of a second, before sliding his hands up her back into her hair and meeting her halfway with the kiss. Their tongues tangled. Their teeth clicked together with unpracticed urgency. His hands were on her ass, then her back, then her hair again. Gayle felt alive in a way she'd hadn't since Ethan's death—since before Liam's birth. Her every nerve ending danced with urgency. The distinct press of Noah's erection against her stomach made her gasp, reach down and unbuckle his belt, unzip his jeans, wanting to feel him in her hand, to understand the reality of this moment. But he stopped her, breaking the kiss and zipping himself back up.

"But...I want..." She reached for him again, feeling like a damned kid in a giant candy store. She'd always been hyper-sexual. It was how she and Ethan had ended up fucking inside his pool house while dozens of company employees partied on the other side of a locked door. She was truly a needy woman, physically speaking. But ever since word had come of the plane crash, her body had gone into total shutdown mode. She hadn't even had the inclination to masturbate, which was something she'd once enjoyed, sometimes once a day. Granted, she'd woken up from some seriously hot dreams about this young man in the past few weeks, but she'd let the moment pass without touching any part of herself. More of her self-inflicted punishment for not being dead along with her son and husband, she supposed.

But now...now...now she wanted him on her, inside her, all over her. It was a little scary how badly she wanted all these things all at once. But given she'd caged her robust libido for exactly three years to this very day, it wasn't terribly surprising.

"God, Noah, please," she whispered, pulling him to her and kissing him until she saw stars. He was a real master at it, she marveled, his skill not lost on her. He liked to tease, nibbling, licking her lips, then plunging in deep, his hands in her hair, his tongue probing and invading her mouth in a way that made her groan and her thighs go weak.

I am, without a doubt, going insane. I'm now even thinking in romance novel language.

He cradled her face between his hands and pressed his forehead to hers. Their breathing was ragged. Gayle wanted to leap out of her clothing and tackle him to the floor. She honestly believed if she didn't get him between her legs in the next five minutes she would implode. He traced her lips with the rough pad of his thumb. She licked it, then bit down on it, making him flinch and grin at her. His face filled her vision and the clean, clear odor of his lust filled her brain.

"Where can we go?" he asked. "Don't you live at your mom's house?"

"Not anymore. I closed on my loft yesterday. Keys are in my purse."

He pulled away from her and ran his hand around the back of his neck. "I don't know, Gayle. I'm not sure you're—"

"So help me, Noah Stokes, if you say I'm not ready one more time..." She placed her hand along the impressive length of his erection under his jeans. "I'm going to go down on my knees right here in my friend's kitchen and show you how ready I am." His eyes shone as he slid one hand up her shirt and cupped her breast, using his other to grip her ass and yank her close so he could grind against her. "That's more like it," she whispered. Her mind tried to recapture her, to shut her down, to remind her this day was for mourning, not for fucking some kid who'd been following her around like a goddamned puppy dog for the last month and a half.

But she jammed the thought aside and leaned back on the island, so he could kiss her neck, tease her nipples, kiss her yet more with those incredible lips. Finally, she pushed him away. "I'm ready for more. Let's go." She grabbed his hand, plucked her purse from the coffee table and headed for the front door. "Evelyn, we're heading out," she yelled up the stairs. Noah yanked her around and pressed her up against the wall, his eager hands up her shirt, his thigh between her legs. "Oh, Jesus," she whispered before he shut her up with a kiss and pinched her nipple so hard she moaned into his mouth and realized she was thrusting her hips forward, rubbing her clit against his thigh right there in the foyer of her friends' house. She closed her eyes and let the small glory of a quick orgasm suffuse her. She was notoriously hair-trigger, coming fast but coming often, which was way better than taking forever and only coming once, she'd always declared.

"Oh...yes..." Noah hissed into her neck, his other hand pulling her higher on his thigh and she rode it, climaxing with gusto and energy she'd forgotten she possessed. "Oh, damn, that was..." He let go of her and pulled his hand out of her shirt, wincing as he tried to adjust himself under his zipper. She smiled, still battling the guilt threatening to overtake her.

"That was just the beginning, I hope." She grinned, amused by his seeming astonishment at her behavior. "I'm still doing the thing on my knees thing. Just later. Come on."

He nodded and followed her out of the door, across the lawn and to her car. She opened the passenger's-side door and he shook his head.

"You drive," he said. "I'm pretty sure I'd have a wreck if I tried to." He grinned at her and got in, tilting the seat back and continuing to adjust himself under the jeans. She stared over at him, wondering at the possibility of what was about to happen, at the sheer unbelievable oddness of it, on this day of all days. He met her gaze. "You all right?" His brown eyes were chocolate-dark with lust.

She swallowed hard, unable to find actual words, and drove them to her new home. It was a short ride and spent in uncomfortable silence. Gayle's nerve endings sang with desire but her brain was beginning to yammer even louder at her, reminding her she was not doing this for the right reasons. Noah was a nice young man and she was about to use him for nothing more than a pure, physical outlet.

But, oh, what an outlet... It was calling her name, screaming it into her ears, demanding she take action, take control, take what she wanted. Because she sensed that Noah was more than willing to give it to her.

"Shut up," she muttered under her breath, parked in the lot under the building and got out. Noah was at her side in a heartbeat, tucking her hair behind her ears, kissing her nose, her cheeks, her lips. She closed her eyes and tried to go back to the amazing place she'd been, but it eluded her. Aggravated, and yet still humming with horny energy, she pushed him off her and hesitated, pressed up against the side of her car in the dark, unfamiliar confines of the underground lot.

He stood with his hands on his hips, chest heaving. "Having second thoughts?" His voice cut through her befuddled haze, forcing aside the encroaching, guilty misgivings about what she wanted to do, about what she wanted him to do to her.

"No," she said, her voice weak. She cleared her throat. "There's the elevator." He grinned and ran for it, beating her there by a few steps. "Sixth floor," she said. The doors slid shut. He touched the stop button and turned to her, hand on his belt buckle. She grinned back at him. "Always wanted a blow job in an elevator, mister?" She let her purse fall to the floor and yanked him forward by his belt loops.

"Nah," he said, as she unbuckled and unzipped him, sighing with relief when his long, elegant cock was released into the stifling hot space. "I've done this plenty of times. You?"

"Nice," she said, stroking him from root to tip, touching across the fluid beading the head then putting her fingertip in her mouth. He tasted of earth, of grass, of the sort of base essence of a man she'd missed without realizing she was missing it. Ethan had been a big fan of this sort of thing, so she'd made sure she gave the best blow job on the planet. "I seriously doubt you've ever had one like this."

He propped his hands on the elevator wall when she slid down his body, pulling his jeans with her so she could get at all of him. Closing her eyes, she took his cock into her mouth, relishing the moment he tensed right before she let the tip hit her throat. He groaned and thrust forward. She released him, keeping one hand under his heavy sac, loving when his balls contracted as she teased around the edge of his head, knowing exactly the right sensitive spots to tantalize before she deep-throated him again. She stroked, letting her finger move back, closer to his ass before she released him again, smiling up into his beet-red face while she stuck her tongue into the cum now beaded up once more.

"Okay, all right," Noah said, his voice breathy.

Gayle tightened her grip on the base of his dick and lapped up all the evidence of his eagerness to climax.

"Fine, fine, you proved your point. But I'm warning you, you'd better stop, if you want me to...holy shit!"

Without a word, she took him deep again, consciously relaxing her throat so he could do exactly what he wanted. At the same moment, she pressed her finger into his ass, having lubed it with his cum.

Noah's hips thrust forward, forcing him deeper into her throat. She breathed through her nose and reached higher inside his ass, finding her target almost immediately "God, god... God!" He shuddered, grunted and came, sending hot liquid down her throat. Gayle closed her eyes and swallowed it, loving the sensation of his raw, primal pleasure, of the way she made him lose control.

He put his hands on her head and withdrew, stumbling backward until he hit the doors, managing to push the number six and release the elevator from its stopped position. Gayle wiped her lips with the back of her hand, zinging from head to toe with pleasure and the sort of erotic anticipation she used to coast along on almost every single day of her life once she'd hooked up with, then fallen in hard love with, Ethan Connolly.

Stop, she commanded herself, closing her eyes not to see Noah's long, still very hard dick. *Do not think about him. Don't even try. It's not fair to anyone, least of all yourself.* She opened her eyes, smiled and stood slowly, amused at the young man's frantic efforts to yank up his underwear and jeans. She stopped him and kissed him, knowing he could taste himself on her lips.

The doors slid open directly into her penthouse condo, already arranged with new furniture, dishes, pillows, sheets and towels. She'd gone more than a tad crazy, spending more money than she'd ever thought possible buying the place with cash and empowering the on-staff decorator at her favorite furniture store to go nuts – to furnish her new space the way she saw fit. The last few days she'd gotten plenty of updates and receipts for money spent. But she'd been too caught up in her three-day ignoring efforts.

She'd been so damn caught up in it, her job, her new life, she'd let this date sneak up on her in a big way. She pushed past Noah, needing water and hoping to shove that tickle of remorse, or guilt, or whatever the hell it was, out of her head. The loft was made up of one enormous room with high, industrial ceilings, and a truly impressive chef's kitchen. Too bad it wasn't going to get much use, unless she hired somebody.

She poured herself a glass of cold water from the fridge door, downed it and refilled it twice before she believed herself prepared to face him. When she did, he'd managed to put his clothes back together but remained near the elevator doors, eying the space warily. "Nice place," he said, not moving. Gayle leaned against the counter and observed him from head to toe, allowing herself a quick memory of the first time she'd laid eyes on him, with his hard hat and power tools and mesmerizing brown stare.

"Thanks," she said, letting him take his time even though her body urged her forward, to let him prove what he wanted to prove to her. "Having second thoughts?" She parroted his earlier, rhetorical question, sipping her third glass of water.

He frowned, shifted from foot to foot, ran his hand around the back of his neck and generally looked way more miserable than a man in his particular position should. The fury began to form thunderheads on the edges of her psyche. When he stayed across the room from her, looking like he wished he could jump back in the elevator and leave, it spilled into her brain, making her speak before she could think.

"Well, I guess you got what you needed. You can go."

He blinked in the face of her harsh tone. She stood straighter, then marched right up to him, anger dulling her senses and her common sense. Putting a hand on his warm chest, she pushed back, keeping him at an arm's length. "I said, you got off in my elevator, so you can leave now."

Noah took her hand and gently put her arm down by her side. "I'm not leaving, Gayle. You know that."

"Fine. Then come in already. Stop gawking like you're at a museum or something. It's a lousy Grand Rapids penthouse condo. It's not a big deal, trust me." She headed for the bedroom, wondering if she'd managed to keep those condoms her mother had given her the night she went out with Evelyn.

"Maybe not to you," he said. Something in his voice made her turn back to look at him. He still hadn't moved from his spot guarding the elevator. She sighed, then took a long breath and smiled. His frown deepened, but it did nothing to lessen the pure, sexy reality of him.

"I'm sorry. I'm not trying to be flippant. Trust me, having all this…" She waved her arms around, attempting to minimize the many thousands of bucks she'd dropped in the last week on this stupid place. "It's not something I was born into. I married into it. Now, I'm not married. You know the whole story. But I *am* horny has hell…so…" She sidled up to him, went up on her tiptoes and wrapped her arms around his neck. He indulged her for a few minutes, ramping up her lust with his killer kissing skills before he took her arms from around his neck and pushed her away.

"Gayle, listen," he whispered. She squirmed, aggravated at his stalling. "I don't know…I mean…I'm not really…." He let go of her and turned away, head hanging low.

"Noah," she said, running her hands up under his shirt to his shoulders and lifting the dark T-shirt over his head. He kept his back to her, which was fine with her since his rear view was as pleasant as any other. "Noah," she repeated before pressing her lips to his shoulder blades, tasting salt, the outdoors and a hint of leather. He remained still, letting her touch his back and arms, shivering when she wrapped her arms around him and teased his nipples before exploring the lovely terrain of his abs.

He was breathing heavily when he turned again, looming over her, but not the way Ethan used to — *stop!* "Stop," she said out loud, slapping her hands over her ears. She felt pulled in a million different directions at once — only one of them with the potential for a happy ending. All the other directions were exerting plenty of pressure, including the dark corner where she'd stuffed anything and everything regarding what had happened to her three years ago today.

Her head pounded. Her ears burned. The rest of her flamed white hot from her scalp to her toes. They stared, unmoving, arms crossed, at apparent impasse. What in God's name was she doing here, with this man, the smell of him all over her, her throat sore from sucking his damn cock?

Granted, he looked just as conflicted as she felt. His brow was furrowed, his lips pressed together, his shoulders hunched. Gayle's knees gave out and she dropped onto the leather couch she'd never seen before walking into this space—her space, she supposed. "Well, shit."

Letting go of the lust that sustained her for the past hour or two not only sucked all the energy out of her, it left her mind free and open to the onrush of memories. She flopped back, hands over her face and gave in to it, let her three-year mental image bank open and spill its guts. Images of Ethan, Liam, of the three of them, of her and Ethan in the early days of their relationship, clogged all her senses. Gayle did nothing to stop them. She couldn't. There was no point. This was her life. She'd been a fool to think otherwise.

The sound of her son's voice, the ghost-memory of her husband's hands on her body, his smile, his laugh, the sensation of her zillion-count Egyptian cotton sheets against her bare skin—it was all fresh, as if it had all just happened to her. This wasn't new. She understood it, could grasp it and realized all she knew how to do was ride it out in her usual fashion.

She stumbled over to what she hoped was the liquor cabinet. Yanking open the doors, she blessed the money spent on having the designer lady prepare her home sight-unseen while admiring all the top shelf booze arrayed in front of her. "Hell yeah," she said under her breath, grabbing the Pappy Van Winkle bottle. "Time to drink," she said, turning and almost running right over Noah. "Excuse me," she said.

He held out his hand. She clutched the bottle to her chest. He snagged it, opened it, took a long slug and handed it back to her. "Well then," she said, knocking back her own drink, shuddering as it burned its way into her chest. "Welcome to my nightmare, Noah Stokes." She waggled the bottle and made her way back to the – to her – couch. He joined her, propped his feet next to hers on the matching leather ottoman and held out his hand. She slapped him a high five.

"No, give me the goddamned bourbon." She took another drink then handed it over, watching him suck back a portion, wipe his lips, then prop the bottle on his thigh. "This is fucked up," he said, putting his arm around her shoulders. She patted his cheek, snagged the bottle back and leaned into him, letting the tears flow.

Chapter Fifteen

Noah had always figured himself for being self-aware. He took particular pride in being honest about his weaknesses as well as his strengths. His recent history aside, he'd always managed to keep to a fairly straight and narrow moral path, especially concerning the members of the fairer sex. Even not putting that aforementioned recent history aside, he'd never once treated a woman badly. If anything, he went out of his way to make sure they felt cherished, treasured, even loved during the time they'd bought and paid for with him. It was ultimately why he'd had to stop doing it — it was too emotionally draining, if physically exhilarating. And, of course, technically illegal.

The odd situation he now found himself in, however, had thrown him for the sort of curve he'd never experienced. The concept that the gorgeous object of his recent obsession had jumped him at her friend's house, kissed him like there was no tomorrow, groped and dry humped him before they left, then treated him to the kind of blow job a man really only fantasizes about was pretty sweet on the one hand. On the other, the fact he'd walked into her gigantic loft home and realized that he wanted—no, he required—more from her than a quick lay had sent him spiraling into his own mind so deep he'd been frozen in his tracks.

And now, of course, they were getting slowly, steadily trashed on a bottle of two-hundred-dollar bourbon, passing it back and forth between them like a paper-bagged Colt 45. Which only added to his general confusion and dismay at his inability to close this particular deal.

"What?" He blinked and realized he'd been staring yet again at Gayle's profile while she drank. The tears she'd been shedding had stopped, but she looked as if she could start them up again at any moment. And no wonder, considering this was the third anniversary of her personal tragedy. He'd known it and had planned for it. Which had made her radio silence of the past three days that much more worrisome. By way of answer to her question, he smiled, tucked a lock of her riotous brown hair behind her ear and touched her lips briefly, before taking the bottle from her and treating himself to another fiery sip.

"Talk to me," he said, handing it back to her. She shrugged, drank and played with the ends of her hair. All distraction mechanisms he'd become familiar with in the past few weeks. It had been a glorious experience, getting to know her via the thrice-a-week hot yoga torture and subsequent snack. Their fun-funny-flirty texts had lifted his spirits every day, while he'd drive from store to bar to store, convincing beer buyers and managers to dump the upstarts and put Fitzgerald products back where they belonged.

Settling into sales flunkey life for the brewery, recognizing the industry was a lot more cutthroat than he'd realized, he still found himself longing for the outdoors. His utterly useless degree in horticultural science—gardening 101, as he used to think of it—seemed even more so now as he got further and further from the life he'd imagined for himself. Years spent digging in the dirt, planting, re-planting, pruning, watering and generally caring for plants, flowers and trees alongside his parents had imprinted on him in a way he couldn't shake. He'd been going on jobs with his father since he was three years old, had learned how various plants took to certain soils, how much or how little to water flower beds, the best way to arrange the decorative grasses and shrubs around a house first-hand, always with the intention of taking over the family business someday. He'd been meant to be the Master Gardner, owner of Stokes Landscaping, happy husband, father, brother, successful pillar of the community. Not this—a washed-up male stripper and part-time prostitute, working odd construction and lawn mowing jobs until he managed to get a gig selling beer.

He sighed, sipped and tugged Gayle down so she was draped over his thighs, relishing the warmth of her body but in a sort of detached, clinical way. She was so broken, yet still so unaware of her own brokenness it amazed him. He stroked her hair when she rolled onto her side and curled into a ball, her hands on his knees. When he tipped the bottle up to his lips and nothing came out, he stared at it, amazed by its empty state. "Shit," he said, tossing it onto the couch next to them. "I don't even feel drunk."

Gayle rolled onto her back and stared up at him. Her hair was spread out beneath her like a silken fan. Her eyes shone. Her face flushed. When she stretched her arms up over her head, her clingy T-shirt moved up, revealing a tempting line of skin. He set his jaw against the temptation and touched her cheek. "Talk to me, Gayle."

"I've had plenty of expensive talk therapy, thanks. Besides, I hardly think you're qualified to—"

"Tell me about Liam," he said. "I want to know more about him."

"I'm… He's…" She blinked fast. A rogue tear slipped out of her eye. He touched the line of wetness on her face and tasted it. She rolled away from him but stayed on his lap, curled into herself again, her hands clutching his knees once more. "I wanted a baby, Ethan's baby, so badly it scared me," she began. "I'd never thought I wanted any kids. But something about…something about Ethan made me change my mind so fast both our heads spun." She sighed. Noah put a hand on her shoulder, hoping to provide reassurance while also encouraging her to go on, to say more. "I never thought I'd fall in love as hard as I did with him, either. So I guess it's fitting."

She stopped. Noah let her have her silence, stroking her arm, shoulder and upper back. He did want to know more about her former life, but he also wanted her to get it out, to lance the wound and let it breathe air so he might find a place in her life beyond the obvious one in her bed.

Resisting the urge to glance toward the room he assumed contained that particular piece of furniture, he smiled when she rolled back over to face him. "I had a bunch of miscarriages. It was a mess. I was a mess. But

I was still working — we both were. It kept us sane, even during the hormone-soaked horror show of those years I spent crying myself to sleep every night over my body's apparent inability to do the one thing it was designed to do." She glanced away from him. "Where's the booze?" He held up the empty bottle. She frowned. "Wow. We should get some water."

"Yeah, okay, but first, tell me more."

She rolled her eyes. He was getting better at ignoring that particular tic of hers. And right now, he felt so comfortable with her he wanted this night to never end. He was hardly a monk, after all, but she had triggered a pretty monstrous climax so he figured he could use another hour to rebuild his stamina. "So, finally, I managed to get and stay pregnant. And this was against my doctor's orders. He wanted me to wait a whole year before we 'tried' again." She hooked her fingers around the word as another tear escaped her eye, giving him another excuse to touch her face. "I was sick of being tired and weepy and Ethan was ready to throttle me if I took my temperature one more time before we had sex. I could hardly blame him. He was ambivalent about kids. This was all on me. Blame biology, or evolution, or whatever. I had to get his kid in me, you know?" She sniffled. Noah handed her a tissue from a conveniently placed box of them on the table beside the couch.

She shook her head. He frowned and held the tissue to her nose until she blew. Once he'd tossed the used hankie on the table, she seemed to have rediscovered a bit of equilibrium. It was another thing Noah prided himself on — comprehending the ever-volatile world of female body language. "Want to sit up?" He held out his hand. She shook her head and put her palm against his cheek. Her touch made his body zing to attention, threatening to send this comfy, cuddly moment into a different zone. "Okay, so...tell me about your son." He glanced over to a set of built-in bookshelves which held several framed photos. "I assume that's him?" He pointed. Gayle closed her eyes.

"Probably. I gave the designer lady one photo — one of the three of us. My mom probably gave her some more."

"He looks like a happy little boy."

"He was. I swear I worried about him because he hardly ever cried or fussed even when he was a newborn." A smile ghosted over her lips. "He was a joy...I didn't want to go back to work even after three months home with him. So, I didn't." She shrugged. "It was also a pretty shocking discovery for me — I'd always pictured myself the busy, working mom with sitters, or a nanny or whatever."

Noah smiled and put a hand on her thigh. When he sensed her shaking, he pulled her up to seated and wrapped his arms around her. "I'll bet you were a great mom. And I'm sure Ethan was a stellar dad. No wonder Liam was always smiling."

She nodded against his neck. "He was so smart. He walked at ten months, was talking complete sentences by his second birthday. Ethan took him everywhere — to the hardware store, to high-level meetings at his company's foundation, you name it. The man was so besotted with that kid. I almost got jealous sometimes." She pulled away from him and stared at him. The rich emerald hue of her eyes was magnified by tears. "I had everything I wanted. But I guess I didn't appreciate it enough. I don't know." She sighed and slumped into him again.

Noah rubbed her back between her shoulder blades until she relaxed. Sensing she'd probably said all she wanted to for the time being, he lifted her chin and kissed her, indulging in one of his favorite forms of foreplay, using his lips and tongue to tell the story he planned to expand upon later. She broke away slowly, her eyes now shining with a different sort of emotion. "You are a damn good kisser. You take lessons or something?"

He grinned and pecked her nose, then pulled her close, loving how comfortable he felt holding on to her, her face mashed against his neck. When her hand landed on his rapidly hardening dick, he chuckled. "What if I told you I did—sort of." She leaned away from him, her lusty expression tinged with skepticism. He'd filled her in on the bare bones of his backstory— the successful, third-generation landscaping business brought to ruin thanks to his father's predilection for betting on shitty horses and being a crappy poker player being the main feature of that. The rest of it— dropping out of school mere months from graduation and hitchhiking his way west, only to find himself employed as a bartender at a strip joint before being 'discovered' and put to work on the stage, and later, on a much smaller stage—he'd kept to himself.

Bolstered by the booze and the promising events of the past few hours, he pushed her off him, found his phone and connected to her loft's wireless with little effort. Gayle curled up and watched him find a good playlist and crank it, sending the chest-thumping R&B song into the high-ceilinged space. He turned away from her to collect himself and channel his former male exotic dancer. Shaking his arms and hands to try to get the feeling back in them, he had a quick thrill of anxiety over what he was about to do. But when the next song played, it was as if the streaming service had read his history—this was *his* song, the one he always used for his first dance. The one that, after about a year spent working out, stripping off his clothes and miming sex, the audience would instantly recognize as the moment he—not Noah, but him with a different, long-forgotten name—would treat them to his dancing and stripping skills.

He smiled, turned around slowly and rolled his hips. Just a little at first, as if he didn't know what he was doing. Gayle frowned at him. He stopped and put his hands on his hips as if embarrassed by his silly effort, waiting for the moment the music broke. When it did, he jerked his head up and met her gaze, holding it for the next three minutes, during which he danced, he stripped and he treated her as if she were the honored guest, the blushing bride at one of the many bachelorette parties they'd hosted.

He picked her up, tossed her legs over his shoulders and pressed his face against her lower belly, then dropped her onto the couch so hard she bounced, giggled, hiccupped and slapped her hand over her mouth as he continued to disrobe in time to the music. Once he was down to his skivvies and sporting a massive tent in them—something he'd never done while a dancer, thanks to the painfully tight jock strap he'd worn to prevent such a thing—he picked her up again, this time encouraging her to wrap her legs around his waist and her arms around his neck. They swayed together, rolling their hips in time to the erotic beat, and kissed until he was dizzy from it, until he knew that if he couldn't get inside her soon he'd spontaneously combust.

The music ended, segueing into something he'd also used for a more energetic dance at one time in his life. "Want more?" he asked, breathlessly holding on to her — not from the dancing but from his gut-deep need to take her into the bedroom and make love for hours, sleep, then wake up and do it some more.

She shook her head, equally breathless. "Not of this little show, if that's what you mean." She smiled, mashed her nose to his, then sucked his lower lip into her mouth. The sensation, while not exactly new, was the most incredible thing he'd ever experienced. It made him ache to be even farther inside her. "Put me down. Please?"

He let go of her and leaned on the high kitchen counter, trying to catch his breath. She poured two glasses of water from the fridge and handed him one.

As he drank, he tried not to be insulted by her apparent lack of being ga-ga over his performance. When he set the glass down, he almost missed the counter, which clued him in to his level of drunkenness. As he was reconfiguring his goals for the next few hours — moving from hours of lively sex and more into the realm of passing out on the couch and praying he would survive the hangover. Before he could get all the way there, however, a Gayle-shaped missile launched itself across the kitchen and into his arms. The force of it made him stumble backward so he kept going until he hit the couch again, dragging her with him.

All the hours, days and weeks he'd spent angling for — fantasizing about — this very minute coalesced into this, into her, or more precisely her lips on his. He clutched at her like some kind of unpracticed rookie, touching her all over, wherever he could find. "You have on way too many clothes," he managed. *Lame. But whatever, since it's true.* Her jeans were irritating him. The very fact of her shirt, her bra, the miniscule pair of panties he finally tugged off her while she lay back on the couch, giggling and hiccupping, pissed him off.

They were drunk. This was a bad idea. But damn him if he wasn't more desperate to get hold of her now than ever.

He loomed over her, one hand on the back of the couch, trying to get his vision to stop wobbling all over the place. "I don't think I've ever had that much straight liquor in…oh…" He smiled when she stretched her arms up over her head, lifting her small but pert breasts. His smile widened as she stretched one long, toned leg alongside him and bent her other one, giving him a clear view of her pussy. "Oh," he said again. "Yes. I forgot to tell you something else." He lowered his lips to her neck and kissed his way down her shoulder, over to one breast, then the other. Her abs were slicked with sweat and he licked them, dipping the tip of his tongue into her belly button.

Her hands were in his hair, twining and tugging, and she lifted her hips, giving him exactly what he wanted. Before he lowered himself to one of his favorite tasks, he rose and met her eager gaze. "What?" She hooked one leg over his shoulder. "Is there a problem?"

"No. But I should warn you…this is something else I'm pretty damn good at. So…you know…"

"Stop talking," she said, her voice husky. "Show me."

Noah had to close his eyes against the onrushing dizziness. God damn it, he did not want their first time to be some kind of a stupid, drunk fuck. He had things he wanted to show her, something to prove.

"Noah," she whispered. He opened his eyes and looked at her once more, the musky scent of her filling his head. He slid to the floor, tugging her around with him and tossed both her legs over his shoulders. "Noah," she repeated. He gripped her ass and lifted her so he could get to work. "Oh…yes," she sighed when he touched his tongue to the sweet nub of plump flesh waiting for him, begging for his attention.

It didn't take long, but he'd dealt with hair-triggers like her before. The problem was, when she cried out and clamped his head between her muscular thighs, coating his face with her juices and gripping the fingers he'd been using to stroke her G-spot while sucking her clit, it triggered something in him. Something that demanded he act. Something a little alarming, but one his drunk brain translated as simple.

"Jesus, Gayle," he said, his voice hoarse, his entire body shaking as her breathing calmed and she rose so she was face-to-face with him. She wrapped her arms around his neck and licked his lips — tasting herself, he knew, when she parted them and probed into his mouth with her tongue. The kiss took on a life of its own, drawing him deeper, further away from the man he'd believed himself to be when he woke up this morning. Closer to the man who wanted her, who wanted to make her smile, to laugh, to be happy — but only with him. The odd possessive surge shocked him, but since he was riding the bourbon express he allowed it to exist in his brain alongside the raw, primal need he had to be inside her ASAP.

With a low groan, he pressed her back, tasting the delicious sweat on her neck and shoulders, sucking at one nipple while stroking the other. "Harder," she demanded. "Harder, damn you."

He obliged, pinching and biting the tips of her breasts.

"Condom," he croaked, before he did something stupid. One of the many things that had stuck with him after his time spent in service of women in exchange for cash was the hard-stop rule of protection. But now, dear God he wanted to slide into her, to thrust hard, just once to experience the velvet grip of her around him without the latex barrier between them.

Yep. I am without a doubt way too drunk for this.

"I don't care. I don't care," she insisted, angling her hips and shifting forward on the couch. "Noah, I want this. Please…" She met his gaze in the split second before she wrapped her legs around his waist and made the last move, the one he'd been holding back from. They groaned in unison at the contact. Noah's brain tried to ping him, to raise the red flag of danger, but Noah had gone away, he figured. Noah was in a super happy place. And he was not going to stop now.

She arched her back, calling his name over and over as he pounded into her, blind and deaf and dumb. This was not how he operated, he tried to remind himself. He didn't just…fuck like this. He was an expert. He provided hours of fun before he allowed himself anything resembling a release. The tight pulse of her climax, combined with the sound of his name followed by "yesssssssss," dragged him right along for the ride.

He gasped, his vision dimmed, then got bright white with the capital-O Orgasm that roared up his spine, hit his brain then dove south, making him grunt with the force of the release. Keeping a tight grip on her hips, he closed his eyes and let himself have it, while his brain waved a million red flags he continued to ignore.

"Noah." The sound of his name again made him open his eyes. He stared down at her, into those huge green eyes that had so captivated him in front of her yoga studio, and something shifted inside him. Something nice, but scary. He let go of her hips, pulled out of her and flopped onto his ass, attempting to process the swirl of emotions that were decidedly too mixed up with liquor. She stretched like a cat, her legs on his lap, her skin shining. He could smell them, the sex, the sweat, the bourbon permeating their pores. Suddenly so exhausted all he wanted was to curl up on the couch and sleep for twelve hours straight, he put a hand on her leg, feeling the muscles under his palm. The muscles he'd been staring at for days and weeks, imagining this very moment. This moment he'd blown — literally — like some kind of eighteen-year-old kid with his first shot at pussy.

"Shit," he muttered, wiping a hand down his face. "I'm sorry."

"Sorry," she said, sitting up slowly and sliding over so she straddled his lap. "For what?"

He smiled up at her, but he was fading and he knew it. He'd been working ten-hour days for Fitzgerald, rounding out his rent money with weekends and a few evenings mowing, pruning, weeding and mulching. But her lips…oh sweet Jesus, her lips were like a slice of heaven. He held on to her, letting his hands slide up her back and into the wild tangle of her hair as he slid into the place he was coming to think of as Gayle-land — a land where he, Noah the sex expert, the highly sought after and just as highly paid gigolo, lost himself so deep he didn't even care he'd come inside her without protection. Gayle-land tasted of honey, of bourbon, of a faint trace of something he assumed was his own cum. It felt soft, yet hard at the same time. It was full of whispers, of promises, of heat.

He pulled away from her, giving her lower lip a quick nip. "Okay, I take it back. I'm not sorry."

She smiled at him, then stood and wobbled her way toward what he assumed was a bathroom. He watched her go, amazed at his luck, appalled by his performance, encouraged by her last kiss. When she emerged and handed him another glass of water, he took it, drank and fell over onto his side.

"God," he croaked. "Can we sleep some so I can maybe redeem myself in the morning?"

A hand touched his shoulder. Lips found his cheek. He reached for her, but only grabbed air. "Come on, lover boy," she said, yanking him up and giving him a tiny shove toward what he assumed was her bedroom. Cursing when he located a table with his shin, he limped toward the door and fell face first into a soft mound of pillows. His last coherent thought was relief that when she crawled into bed with him and he pulled her close so he could bury his face in her hair, she sighed and pressed back against him, still muttering his name.

Chapter Sixteen

Gayle had experienced plenty of hangovers in her life. More than she cared to admit, most days. She considered herself pretty well expert in the tricks to avoid them, short of not drinking at all. Plenty of water, sleeping past the point her body had simply passed out, a solid breakfast the next day to soak up the residual booze in her system. But really, knocking back an entire bottle of way-overpriced bourbon in one sitting, then getting her brains bonked out by the hot and studly kid lying next to her? That did demand the sort of head-clanging agony she woke with the next morning.

The room was so bright when she did open her eyes it felt like there were lights shining right down on her, making her sweaty under their unwavering glare. She tried to roll over and tug the sheet up, to escape into a bit of sleep, to perhaps ease past the worst of it. But when her nose mashed up against Noah's broad back, a rush of nausea forced her out of bed and toward the porcelain god. After a few minutes spent in gut-heaving worship, she brushed her teeth and drank about a gallon of water straight from the bathroom tap.

Way to christen the new place, Gayle. Truly classy.

When she met her own eyes in the massive mirror over the sink, she couldn't help but notice the way her lips seemed swollen. Smiling at the somewhat hazy memory, she turned her head and frowned at the line of tiny hickeys down her neck. When her arm grazed her left breast, she flinched and gave a squawk of pain. Glancing down, she noticed both her smallish nipples were also swollen-looking, redder than usual, and sore when she touched them.

And it wasn't the only place she was sore. She shifted from foot to foot, recognizing the oh-so-pleasant pain centered between her legs. She decided a hot shower was in order, and spent a solid half hour there, using shampoo, soap and hot water to try and revive herself. But as always, it only resulted in transforming her into a much cleaner, but still woefully hung-over human.

As she dried off, a noise from the bedroom made her peek around the corner, embarrassed as she accepted the hard fact she'd acted like a total slut last night, at least when she hadn't been sobbing her stupid head off. Noah had rolled onto his back and had his arm over his eyes. The million-thread-count sheets she must have paid for at some point during the condo outfitting frenzy had slipped to his upper thighs. In an instant, the embarrassment faded, leaving behind a white-hot flush of horniness.

Taking a minute to appreciate the masculine work of art spread out on one side of her new bed, she couldn't help but smile at her luck.

Dude's an ex-stripper? Bonus points for me.

As if sensing her eager gaze, his long, elegant dick stirred and hardened as she watched, causing a corresponding sensation between her own legs. With the sound of her rapidly increasing breath in her ears, she touched herself, her fingertip finding the eager bud of her clit in seconds. She touched her sore nipple, then pinched it, making her knees weak and a small sound escape her throat.

God, but he'd been hot last night. Gyrating around her living room loft, picking her up, kissing her then shedding his clothes bit by bit, like the pro he apparently was — it'd almost made her come in her jeans. Of course, the whole thing had given her a short pause, one that would likely have called a halt to the whole thing had she been sober. Her Noah — the young man who'd been so sweet, helpful, polite, gentlemanly and, of course, painfully handsome when he'd been paying a sort of old-fashioned court to her the past few weeks — he was this…this sex god, used to cavorting around on stages for money?

Even as her mind made this journey, her finger moved faster and her breathing got faster. His dick — truly a work of art and longer than she'd personally ever seen or experienced — was rigid now. A small bead of liquid appeared at the tip. She grinned wider and spread her legs, needing a quick release so she could dive in there and provide him with the same. She closed her eyes and let it happen, a tiny squeak of pleasure accompanying her skin's heat and the small rush of fluid coating her upper thighs.

When she opened her eyes, Noah was up on his elbows, his eyes gleaming, his cock still ramrod hard. She licked her lips and stood straighter.

"Gosh, lady, you sure are hot," he said, his voice low, his fake-naïve words making her smile. "I love a woman who knows how to pleasure herself." He crooked a finger at her. "But you know what I love more?"

She made her way over to him, sitting and taking the heat of him in her hand. As she stroked, he reached out to cup her breast, passing his thumb over her erect nipple. "What?" she asked, unable to take her eyes off the sculpted perfection of his torso. "Tell me what you love more, Noah." She had a recollection of screaming his name the night before—screaming it a lot. But she adored the way it rolled off her tongue. She wanted to caress it, the way she was caressing his beautiful cock right now.

"I love it when a woman says my name when she comes."

She smiled at him, her heart doing a strange sort of flip in her chest. His eyes—that amazing shade of golden brown—were open, honest, guileless, if she were to use a ten-dollar word for them. They were full of something she recognized and wasn't sure she wanted to see—at least not yet. And yet her body urged her forward, the way it used to do before.

"Well," she said, crawling up his body and dropping down to touch her tongue to the well-defined muscles of his abs, to his nipples, to his neck then to his lips. "I'm two for two then." She licked his lower lip, then his upper one. He let her, staying propped on his elbows as they kissed. It was slower, easier, a more familiar thing this morning. His lips were something she knew now and understood. They explored each other, their mouths the only thing touching. His breathing was ragged when she pulled away and ran her hand down his chest, his stomach, stopping when she wiped the pre-cum from his dick and put her finger in her mouth.

He grinned, his tousled hair and somewhat sleepy expression making her do that weird heart-flip thing again. *Cut it out*, she admonished herself. *This is nothing but a distraction, something I need, something he wants. Enjoy it and don't read anything into it. Never mind the fact I spent the third anniversary of my husband's and son's deaths screwing around with this...this...amazing specimen.*

"All right, Gayle, it's time." He rose fast and flipped her onto her back. She giggled, then sighed with satisfaction when he put what was no doubt another line of hickeys down the other side of her neck. The sun streamed into her new loft bedroom, which only added to the surreal sensation of Noah—her Noah—and his painfully pleasurable attention to every inch of her skin here, in the nest of expensive sheets in a bed she'd not seen before last night.

After making her writhe and moan and demand he touch her pussy while he'd been licking, sucking and tugging at her nipples, he stopped. She sighed, anticipating he'd move the mouth party southward, and bent one knee, letting the other fall to the side. But he sat, crouched back on his heels, a pensive expression on his face.

She was practically humming with need by now. Her ears were all white noise. Her skin flushed. Her body trembling and requiring more. But he didn't move. Only sat, studying her with that borderline unhappy look on his face.

She went up on her elbows. "What's wrong? I don't do it for you anymore?"

He frowned and flopped onto his butt, crossing his legs as if ready for a chat, which made the fact of his rigid erection somehow ironic. He seemed miserable, which was beyond her, since they'd had a ton of fun the night before and were about to do more of the same. She sat, mirroring him, and lifted his chin so he had to look at her. "What is it?"

"I don't think I can do this," he said. She blinked and looked straight at his cock, which was more than capable, then back up at him. "That's not what I mean."

"Noah, you're overthinking." She reached for him, still eager and thrumming with urgency.

"No, I'm not. And besides, I need a rubber."

She flinched, recalling how she'd begged him the night before, of how nicely he'd obliged her begging, coming so hard she'd felt the warmth of him spilling inside her. A small touch of anger lit the edges of her consciousness. Unwilling to ruin this, she shoved it down under a pile of lust. "I want you," she said, simply. "You want me, I think. We're consenting, single adults. What's the problem?"

He ran a hand down his face. "I don't know. I'm…you're…it's…I don't want to be this boy toy thing for you, Gayle." His eyes were so full of emotion she was able to suppress the giggle at the very term she'd been using in her head about him. "I want more from you. And I don't know if you can give it to me."

Unable to contradict this and unwilling to bullshit him, she reached out and stroked his stubbly cheek. He closed his eyes, grabbed her hand and kissed her palm. "Tell you what," she said, moving closer, pleased when he didn't seem to object. "Why don't we take this one day at a time?" She took his hand and pulled him forward where she lay back, loving the heavy warmth of his body against hers. "It's just our first time, you know? And you can rest assured I'm going to want to see you again."

She was going to want a lot more, now that he'd woken her inner horn-dog. She smiled at him, moving her hips and wrapping her legs around his waist, loving how he groaned when his hard dick pressed against her pussy. She moved, finding the friction she wanted against her clit as he stared down at her, his eyes still clouded with doubt.

"I don't know…" he said.

"I do. And I think this will be nice, for both of us. If you'll let it be, I mean."

"You don't know me, Gayle." She moved faster, thrusting against the head of his cock. His eyes shone. "I need more. I'm going to ask more from you."

"Noah," she yelped. "Oh God, baby, please."

He made a small movement with his hips, going so deep it made her gasp, while keeping his pubic bone pressed to her eager clit. "Come on me, Gayle," he said, his voice low, growly and so sexy, she did, just like that, crying his name while her body clenched and released, her nerve endings dancing through another glorious climax.

"Jesus," she sighed, looking up at him. He was still balls-deep inside her. His jaw was clenched, his face red. "You're amazing," she said, reaching back to grip the top of the headboard so she could lift her hips higher. "So fucking amazing." To her surprise, tears burned her eyes and slipped down her cheeks. He leaned down and licked them away, stopping at her lips so she could taste the salt.

His hips began to move, slowly, rolling, like the dance moves he'd treated her to the night before. The primal sensation of his cock pulling out and thrusting back into her body brought her straight back to the edge. He looked down at where their bodies were joined, then back into her eyes. "You're amazing," he said, his voice clear now, but still in the lower, lusty octave. "I thought that the minute I saw you the first time. I've been wanting to do this," he said, giving his first hard thrust, shift her up on the pillows. "And this," he growled, doing it again, making her groan with pleasure. "And this." He sat up on his knees and grabbed on to her hips, digging his fingertips in deep. If it were possible to feel him even deeper, she did, and while it had a painful edge to it, the raw joy of the moment negated it. "Oh God, Gayle…" He groaned and thrust again, again, going faster and still faster.

She bent one leg, noting how his thrusts took on a serious rhythm at the slight change of angle. He let go of her hips and fell forward, his body pounding into hers fast, hard, and needy. She wrapped her arms around his neck and put her lips to his ear. "Come, Noah. Fill me up, baby. I want it. I want it now."

He groaned so loud she felt it in her chest as he did what she said, filling her, her body reacting by treating her to another small release. They clung to each other for several minutes after their hips had stopped moving. "Kiss me," he said. She leaned away from his neck and slanted her lips over his, realizing and accepting at that moment she was a goner. That she'd give this amazing man anything he wanted…as long as he didn't demand her heart. Not because she didn't want to, but because it was simply no longer hers to give. It had turned to dust. Dust she'd tossed over the balcony of her empty house overlooking the Pacific Ocean.

Chapter Seventeen

Six weeks later

"You won't regret it, Stan," Noah said, grinning at Kevin, the TriCities sales guy. He grinned back.

"*I owe you one,*" Kevin mouthed when the regional buyer for a huge grocery chain turned away to address an employee's interruption.

Noah nodded, mentally high-fiving himself over today's victory when Kevin entered the sale into his hand-held computer. It truly was a major coup, since the store had been monkeying around with their craft shelves and some of the bigger players, including Fitzgerald Brewing, had been shoved to the hinterlands. In the cases of some stores, Fitzgerald had been usurped altogether. Which was one of the reasons he'd been added to the sales roster — to be another set of eyes on the rapidly changing beer horizon on behalf of one of the most successful Michigan-based breweries.

When his phone buzzed in his pocket, he realized the very sensation of it—of the distinct vibration against his thigh—was making his dick hard. "Hang on a sec, Kev. I need to check this." Face hot, he pulled the device out and stared down at the message *du jour*.

I'm in the mood for dancing tonight.

"Hey, Noah," Stan the grocery guy said, breaking into the insta-fantasy invoked by Gayle's message. "Can I ask you about something?"

"Sure, sure thing. Give me a quick second. Gotta handle something on the home front real quick." He rolled his eyes, indicating their mutual camaraderie as men with regards to the ladies in their lives.

As if, he thought, typing out a quick reply.

Sounds like a plan to me. Meet you there, 10:30?

He stared at the screen, watching the little 'I'm answering' bubbles flashing. His face got even hotter once her words populated the screen.

Actually, I have a surprise for you.

The last surprise she'd treated him to had involved a private jet, caviar and champagne, and him joining the mile-high club before they spent a sex-soaked weekend on some beach. It had been their first weekend together, which had been followed by more decadent, amazing experiences than he'd ever had—which had been a damn high bar to breach. The common thread was money. Trips, private jets, hotel suites, shopping trips to 'fill out his wardrobe'—all of it wrapped around some of the most erotic sex he could possibly imagine.

Any man in his position would be thrilled. A gorgeous, virile, rich-as-hell woman at his fingertips, all the sex he could ever want, plus gifts? Pretty sweet set-up, he figured.

So, what was his problem?

As he typed out his answer, he tried to suppress the low-lying anger he'd been nursing for the past ten days.

If it involves another weekend away, I'll have to get a raincheck. I have two events to cover for Fitzgerald.

He waited a beat, then softened it with—

Sorry. But I'm down for the nightclub. You know I'm always up for a night of dancing with you, sexy.

Her response made his ears burn. He turned further away from the two men behind him, who were chatting and waiting for him to handle his home front business.

Take the weekend off. I know your boss. I'll write you a note.

Jaw clenched, he let the anger spill over into his next message.

Gayle, I have to work. I want to work. Can't it wait? I'm free next weekend.

When the little answer-bubbles didn't appear, he figured he'd pissed her off. It wouldn't be the first time. The first week after the night—and the whole next day—spent in her condo he'd toyed with her a little, figuring she'd like it. But after he'd ignored her for a forty-eight-hour period, she'd showed up at his tiny cubicle at Fitzgerald dressed in her short skirt, silky blouse and sky-high patent leather shoes after having 'a quick meeting' with his bosses.

He'd swiveled his seat around and leaned back, hands behind his head, his body revving into the highest possible gear at the sight of her. He'd been dreaming about that night for so long, it still felt unreal to him, despite how sore his dick, or how scratched his back was. "Hi there," he'd said, more than aware of all the eyeballs on him and the sex-on-a-stick woman most of them knew as the slightly ball-busting new sales director at TriCities glaring down at him.

"Come with me," she'd said, before tuning on those fuck-me pumps and heading for the front door.

"Mama's calling, junior," some snide asshole had quipped.

"I'd follow her anywhere."

"Dude, are your fuckin' legs broken or what?"

Without a glance at any of them, he'd gotten up and followed her to the door, and to the parking lot where she already stood next to her giant German-made car, arms crossed, one toe tapping impatiently. He'd stopped several feet away from her, his innate sense of irritation fighting a losing battle with his inner seriously horny man. She'd looked devastating, so god damned fuckable it had taken all he had not to flip her around and bend her over the hood of the Mercedes.

"You drive," she'd said, opening the passenger door and climbing him, giving him a breathtaking view of her thigh. He'd hesitated. When the horny man won the arm wrestling match, he'd climbed in behind the wheel, blind and deaf to anything but her—including the fact he'd just waltzed out of his office forty-five minutes early without shutting down computers or anything else.

"Where're we going?"

"Your place," she'd said, resting her hand on his thigh when he pulled onto the interstate.

He'd laughed. "Bullshit. My place is a pit. One step up from a roach motel." It wasn't quite that bad, but he wasn't about to take her there.

"I don't care," she'd said, letting her hand slide up toward his crotch. He shifted to make room for his hardening cock. "Take me there. I want you to fuck me in your bed."

"Okay," he'd said. And he'd done it—several times. They'd ended the night on his ratty couch watching Netflix and eating popcorn. When he'd woken with her in his arms, both of them tangled in his clean but threadbare sheets, he'd experienced such a rush of happiness he'd let her call all the shots for the next few weeks.

But he'd been coping with a burgeoning sense of frustration over her unwillingness to do anything more than fuck. Not that he was complaining. But in a way, he was. Which only caused his frustration to make a full circle. He was obviously the woman's boy toy, her plaything, her walking dildo. She called, he ran. She said jump, he asked if he could eat her out before he leapt.

It was fun, of course. Their libidos matched in a way that was a bit eerie. They'd had sex in her office—one memorable late night he'd surprised her by showing up with a pair of handcuffs, a crop and a bottle of cheap champagne. They'd had sex in her car, in the large beer cooler at TriCities — twice. They'd fucked on a plane, on the beach, in the pool, in various showers and her tub. It was amazing, incredible, any man's fantasy.

But he was done. At least the way she was playing it. He loved her and he suspected she felt the same way about him. When they weren't fucking they were eating, drinking, talking, laughing. She'd told him more about both Ethan and Liam. He'd told her about his months spent as a high-priced male prostitute, fulfilling fantasies for lots of wealthy women. They'd shared everything. But yet, she was holding back in a way that made him want to put both his fists through the wall.

"Noah?"

"Yeah, sorry." He tucked his phone away and refocused on his day job.

"Women, huh?" Stan slapped him on the back so hard he coughed.

"Yeah." His ears were still ringing with fury. He should stand her up. Let her cool her damn heels for a while so she'd be forced to come to him and ask what was wrong. But he knew he wouldn't. Even now the tip of his cock was tingling in anticipation and his skin prickled with the memory of her touch.

Chapter Eighteen

When he showed up at the nightclub, dressed in tight black jeans and one of the shirts she'd bought him when they'd gone on a 'quick junket' to Italy, the place was in full-throated party roar. He fended off plenty of admiring glances and a few overt passes while he waited at the private table he'd been directed to by the head bouncer. As he sipped his beer and people-watched, it became clear to him she wasn't going to show, despite her having reserved this table and instructed he be seated at it.

When a woman who could have stepped right out of a high fashion photo shoot approached him, her full, reddened lips parted in a smile, he had an inkling what she had planned for him. The woman slid into a seat and poured herself a shot of the chilled vodka – Gayle's hard liquor of choice. Sipping, she kept her gaze on him. When she crossed her long, tan, legs he allowed himself a full look at her. She had huge tits – something Gayle couldn't lay claim to – a slim waist and legs that went on forever. She was hot as fuck, truth be told. And the fact of her — that he knew damn well what she was there for — made him shiver.

Gayle had done this once before and he'd happily played along. But he was not in the mood for her games tonight. He was sick and tired of being played like goddamned violin. "I'm sorry you wasted your time tonight. I hope she paid you well." He drained his beer and got up, furious, and yet so eager to lay eyes on her he believed he could claim the honor of being most pussy-whipped idiot on the planet. "I'm leaving."

"Wait," the woman said, putting her hand on his thigh to stop him. "Settle down. Have another beer."

"I don't want another beer," he said through clenched teeth.

"Okay. Let's dance then." She rose, letting her breasts brush against his arm. Her breath was warm in his ear. "I hear you're a damn good dancer." Her hand rested on his ass. He glared down at her, then took her arm and yanked her none-too-gently down the steps to the dance floor. She wanted a fucking show — he would, by God, give her one she'd never forget.

He turned to the girl and smiled at her. "What's your name, hot stuff?"

"Kat," she said, licking her lips and gyrating to the chest-thumping music.

"Nice," he said, matching her movements. "Suits you," he whispered in her ear before biting her earlobe once. "Show me what ya got, Kitty-Kat."

She blushed, which made him horny. Which a good thing, he figured, since he'd be performing with the lovely Kitty-Kat tonight, for an audience. After about an hour spent simulating sex masquerading as dancing, he was so revved he could've fucked Kat right on the dance floor.

"Come on," he said, tugging her away from the sweaty scrum and heading for the private party area for part two of the night's festivities. Fury at Gayle's machinations mingled with the smoky cloud of lust he was floating through as he pushed people aside and ducked into the back room with its separate bar, its dark corners, its waiting audience.

Kat was as eager as he was to get down to business. He located his usual room and pressed her up against the wall, kissing her, groping her ass, her killer tits, all the while getting angrier. When she bit his lower lip and said, "Hey, hot stuff, look over there," he let go of her and turned to find Gayle sitting in a lounge chair, holding a beer and smiling at them.

"You know what, fuck you. Fuck both of you." He sighed. "Sorry, Kat. This isn't your fault." He kept his gaze on the woman dressed all in black, including those heels he loved for her to wear when he'd fuck her standing up, something he'd likely done in this very room. She sipped and kept her gaze neutral as he fumed and willed his cock to soften so he didn't look like such a dork in front of her. "I am done playing games," he said. "Done. You can take your dominatrix, bossy, rich-bitch bullshit and shove it up your ass. Excuse me," he muttered under his breath as he shouldered his way past Kat. He'd made it all the way to the door between the private and the public parts of the nightclub when Gayle yelled his name. He ignored her and kept going. He was done with this. He might be nuts, but being this sort of kept sex toy was not what he wanted from her.

"Noah, hang on a second, please." The tone of her voice—less pleading and disappointed in his refusal to perform and more honest frustration—made him freeze. But only for a few seconds. There was one way to put an end to this. He had to do it, as much as he didn't want to.

He'd made it all the way home before true regret set in. *What have I done?* He'd spent so many days and weeks trying to finagle himself into the very position he had right now. *God, I'm an idiot.*

He unbuttoned his shirt, shed his shoes and grabbed two beers from his fridge before settling onto the couch with a late-season baseball game on the TV. "Screw this," he said, downing the first beer fast and opening the second. "And screw her." And he would, too, if she showed up at his door.

He woke with his face stuck to the arm rest and his neck bent at a painful angle. Wiping the dried spit off his cheek, he sat and tried to figure out where he was and what in the hell time it was. The TV was still on, blaring a mindless infomercial. All his lights were off, which made the room glow silvery blue from the screen. He reached for his phone on reflex and saw Gayle had sent one text, about an hour ago.

I'm sorry. Can we please talk? I'll be at the Brew Corner tomorrow. Our usual table.

He groaned, got up and limped to the bedroom, deciding that to answer her would only make the inevitable worse.

* * * *

The next morning, he went to work, then hit the gym hard after. The solid two-hour cardio and weight regimen kept him focused away from the fact that Gayle hadn't said another word to him via text — her preferred method of communication. The next day was Friday and he spent the bulk of it on the road with distributor sales reps, selling, glad-handing, the usual. He felt like an automaton. But it turned out to be a pretty fruitful day.

He went to the gym again, realizing he'd been looking forward to their usual Friday night spent at a fancy restaurant, drinking expensive cocktails, sharing a steak and conversation. To be followed by quality time at her place — something that always made him feel weird. But he never let it quell his need for her, which only got more intense every time they made love.

When he accepted she wasn't going to ask him again, he sent her a text.

I need ice cream. Meet you at the usual place?

She didn't reply. Figuring that the wanting ice cream part was true enough, he took a shower and headed out, hair still damp, brain spinning with his own stupidity. He missed her. And not just her body. He was, without a doubt, the weakest asshole on the planet.

Their usual place was a Dairy Queen near downtown. It was full old-school, with food and booths in addition to the usual air-bubble-riddled ice-cream-like products. He parked and got out, smiling at the gaggle of college student girls who eyeballed him, while checking for Gayle's car. With a sigh, he headed inside, ordered his favorite — a cookie-dough Blizzard — and took a seat by the window. Some guy with a bald head and broad shoulders was one table over, working away at a banana split while he read something on his computer tablet. Noah nodded when the guy met his eyes, then looked out of the window, wondering how in the world he might salvage this thing with Gayle while somehow retaining his manhood at the same time. About halfway through the overly sweet garbage in his cup, he realized he might be willing to forgo the manhood part, just for a shot at talking to her again.

"You Stokes?" The bald dude was now standing at his table.

Noah glanced up at him, irritated at the interruption. "Yeah. Who's asking?"

Baldie held out his massive paw of a hand. "Name's Hettinger. Trent Hettinger."

Noah shook his hand but tried to give off a 'get the fuck away from me, I'm pining for my Cougar Mama' vibe. It didn't work. "Mind if I join you a second?"

Noah nodded and the guy slid into the booth across from him. "Are you the Stokes of Stokes Landscaping?"

"Yeah. Not that it matters anymore." He took another bite, grimacing at the ersatz sweetness.

"Okay, so…" The guy punched something up on his tablet then turned the screen around so Noah could see it. He squinted at it, trying to figure out why this guy was showing him photos of his grandfather's once-successful business.

"If you have this, you know why I'm sitting here, not running this business." He shoved the tablet back across the table. "What's your point?"

"I'm interested in buying it."

Noah sipped from a cup of water, almost choking on it at the sound of that little news flash. "Buying it? It's not for sale. I mean…the government owns it now — for the taxes and crap."

Trent grinned at him and closed the tablet. He leaned on the table, his dark gaze intent. "I own several retail blocks here in GR, and one in Kalamazoo. I also have a couple of liquor stores and a coffee shop. But I've always wanted to get into landscaping. Those guys make a goddamned fortune, at least the ones I've been paying to handle my properties do."

"Good for you. What does it have to do with me?" He got up and threw away the half-eaten Blizzard, stopping to refill his water and ponder this odd encounter. Standing, he hoped to relay the message he was done talking and had no desire to dredge up all the reasons Stokes Landscaping no longer existed.

Trent turned to face him, obviously not getting the message. "I want to get it out of hock and put you back in charge of it."

Noah frowned. He wasn't in the mood for fairy tales. "You can't do that. I mean, it'll take at least three quarters of a mil to pay off all the tax liens. And the damn place is a wreck. It'll take another…oh…two-fifty at least to clean it up and get the equipment running again."

"No problem," Trent Hettinger claimed, sticking his hand out again. "I'm so happy to have you on board."

"Whoa, dude, I never said…what? You can pay all that?"

"I can. And I've already started the process."

Noah slid into his seat again, his knees suddenly weak. "How…how did you know where to find me?"

"We have a mutual friend."

Noah groaned and dropped his head onto his hands.

"She must really like you a lot. And she knows I was looking to expand into landscaping, so she sent me the info and told me…" He shrugged, looking sheepish. "She told me you'd be here."

"Great." Noah rose, anger filling his chest and threatening to spill out of his mouth. "Good luck with it, Mr. Hettinger. You'll need it."

"Wait, Noah," the guy said, as he was turning away. "I'm serious. This isn't bullshit. I want to buy it and put you in charge."

"Well, if you'll pardon my French, fuck you," he said, tipping an imaginary hat to the man. "And you can give Gayle the same message for me."

Chapter Nineteen

"You are certifiable."

Gayle nodded and stared into her coffee, her chest tight with anxiety. "I know. But...I thought he'd want it, you know?"

"What else have you bought him?" Evelyn sipped her lemon-choked water while the two women sat in the Brew Corner coffee shop the Monday after her abortive attempt to convince Noah she only had his best interests at heart. In the stupidest possible way, she now realized.

"Well..." She traced a line of spilled salt on the table.

"Jesus, Gayle."

"I know, I know. It was stupid. But I...he...shit."

"Well, is it over now?"

"Probably." She sighed and looked around, recalling their many hours spent here, laughing and talking in between bouts of energetic sex. "Crap."

"Do you love him?"

She blinked, then stared at her friend. "I can't... I mean..."

Evelyn grabbed her hand and held on tight. "I know you think you can't. But I haven't seen you as happy as you've been for the past few weeks in so long."

"I don't deserve to be happy."

"Will you just stop?"

Gayle glared across the table. "You have no right to tell me anything about this."

"You know what? I think I do." She put down her glass with a *thunk* and leaned forward on her elbows, her blue eyes blazing with something Gayle thought might be anger. It wasn't as if her friend didn't have it in her. In fact, Evelyn Fitzgerald's temper was legendary in some circles. The woman suffered few fools and even fewer whiners.

But...aren't I entitled to a little whining? Have I not earned the right to feel confusion, even frustration regarding my emotions when it comes to men? Jesus. Cut me some slack.

Evelyn grabbed her hand, surprising her out of her self-righteous reverie. "Listen to me, Gayle Connolly." Her grip tightened when Gayle tried to wriggle out of it, unwilling to hear a lecture, even if it might very well be deserved. "You've been through hell. The sort of hell no wife or mother should have to experience. But you're in a different place now. I can tell you are. I've known you almost my whole damn life. I supported your whole move-to-California thing and celebrated all the amazing things that happened to you once you did." She paused. Gayle was shocked to see tears in her friend's eyes, which of course triggered her own. "And I mourned with you when you lost everything. I love you. I'm here for you." She let go of Gayle's slightly numb hands and sat back in her chair, her lips set in a firm line. "Which is why I'm fully justified in saying this now — it's time to get your head out of your ass."

The self-righteousness rose in her again as she flexed her fingers. "My head is not — "

Evelyn lunged forward again. "Yes. It is. I think you think you're doing the right thing. You mean well taking Noah on like…like some kind of a project. But he's a man. A grown man with a heart to go with…the rest of him." She raised an eyebrow. Gayle could barely stop the giggle before it burst out of her. "And from what I can tell — and you know I know all, over there at the brewery with my family's name on it — he is miserable right now."

"I told you. I tried to fix it." Gayle's voice sounded weak even to her, which was something she hated. She and Evelyn had grown up dirt poor but had both managed to right themselves, to find happiness, love, success in spite of their crappy start in life. Weakness was something neither of them could tolerate, especially in themselves. Gayle had been reminded more than once this was both a strength and a liability. Ethan used to get so furious with her when she'd go off on a tear about some employee, or brewery rep, or store manager or another for what she deemed 'sheer fucking incompetence'.

"You can be an intolerant bitch sometimes," he liked to say. And he'd say it mildly, while doing something else, as if it weren't a giant insult. *"Lighten the fuck up, darlin'. Your life isn't so damn bad. And remember, not everybody is as lucky as you."* He'd follow it up with a hug, a kiss, a fondle, which almost always led to sex.

Gayle closed her eyes against the next thing that would happen when she put the words 'Ethan' and 'sex' together in her head. But instead of his lips, hands and body, she got Noah's. Something new, wonderful, recent and, she realized, something she missed very much right now.

"God damn it," Evelyn muttered, rising, hand over her lips. "I'll be right back." Her friend made her wobbly way to the bathroom and Gayle fought back the urge to scream, something that wouldn't go over well in this crowded hipster coffee bar her friend Trent owned. Instead, she focused on all the kids in the place. Babies filled strollers or got nursed at various tables. Toddlers babbled, fussed, laughed and ran around the place willy-nilly. Moms and dads and more than a few grandparents bought them yogurt or donuts or whatever they wanted, followed them around, tried to have conversations around it all.

When the sight of it didn't make her want to cry more, she realized something. She sighed and stared out of the window, pondering the odd moment for a few seconds. A hand touched her shoulder, but she didn't move. Lips grazed her ear, but she didn't flinch. A voice—an oh-so-beloved, familiar deep voice filled her consciousness. *"Go, Gayle. Be happy for a change. It's what we want for you."*

She shook her head, squeezed her eyes shut, and dropped her hands into her lap, twining her fingers together, determined to ignore it. But the voice, Ethan's voice, kept saying to her, *"Go. Be happy."*

"I will never be happy," she whispered through her clenched jaw. "I won't. I won't. I *won't*." But her heart wasn't pounding. Her pulse didn't race. No tears threatened. She felt somehow light, or lighter than usual while this bizarre thing happened to her in the middle of a crowded coffee joint in her hometown.

She sensed Ethan's hand on her back. It made her feel safe. She wanted to lean into him, to make him hold her one more time. To tell him she was sorry for being such a silly, temperamental bitch about the private plane thing. What had happened to her husband and son on that plane had been a total fluke of the air, the weather, of fate. It had nothing to do with the soundness of the plane.

"*I love you,*" Ethan's voice said. "*I love you, Gayle, but if you don't stop being such a crazy cow right now, you're going to lose something you deserve – another shot at life.*"

"I don't *want* a life without you and Liam," she insisted, loudly in her head and whispered from her lips.

"*But you have one and you'd better get the fuck up off your ass and live it.*"

Gayle glanced at the ceiling, smiling at her dead husband's plain-spoken manner. She missed it, along with everything else, even his mule-headedness. Noah wasn't exactly as forthright — okay, brusque was a better word for it. Noah was even-tempered, calm, yet firm — so different from Ethan, from what she'd lost. But it was soothing in a way Ethan had never been. Life with Ethan had contained plenty of sharp edges. They were almost too much alike sometimes. Noah...he was more of a complement, a completion, filling in her personality holes while she did the same for him.

But he was so damn young. Wouldn't people talk about them? Snigger behind their hands at her, the cougar-y widow with her hot stud by her side.

Who the fuck cares? The man is my equal. And I...I might just love him.

Sighing, she leaned slightly to one side, imagining Ethan there, his strong arms around her, his lips pressed to her hair. *"Go, Gayle. Be happy. I mean it."*

"How's Liam?" she whispered, glad Noah had spent some time forcing her to talk about him so she could mourn him properly.

"Go," Ethan repeated instead of answering her. *"We love you, honey. But we need for you to move on."*

And just like that, the strange, ghostly moment was over. Evelyn had shown up at some point and sat, sipping and watching her. "You all right?"

Gayle nodded, glancing at her over-priced, untouched coffee, now gone stone cold in front of her. "I...I need to go." She got up slowly.

Evelyn smiled at her and held out her hand. Gayle took it, never more grateful for her friend's steady presence.

"Good luck," Evelyn said. "But go easy on him. Don't be so...bossy."

Gayle flushed hot, recalling how much he bossed her, at least behind closed doors. A sudden surge of panic filled her chest, blooming up into her throat. "I...I gotta fix this."

Evelyn dropped her hand and picked up her glass. "Keep me posted. Our Labor Day picnic is coming up. I'll need to know if you're bringing your plus one." She winked. Gayle rolled her eyes and headed for the door, intent, yet worried she might well be too late.

Chapter Twenty

When Gayle's text message hit his phone, Noah wanted to ignore it. He fully intended to ignore it. He was busy anyway, calf-deep in mud and chaos. He and Trent were walking the property that had once showcased acres of flowering and decorative trees alongside the massive greenhouses of his family's landscaping business. He'd agreed to do this, more out of a sense of obligation than anything. But when he'd arrived here, the years of memories he'd been suppressing flew to the surface, nearly smothering him in nostalgia and no small amount of anger at his useless old man.

"This is great," Trent was gushing at every turn, as Noah explained to him the various profit centers the company had boasted. His great-grandmother had been the one to figure out sustaining a large family on a seasonal business wasn't tenable, so she'd concocted the service side—the mower, tractor and other implement tune-ups, the mower blade sharpening, which in this climate had also doubled for skate blades. She'd started and run it. After five years, it had become a cash cow, almost surpassing their other lucrative services.

"Yeah, great," he said, noting the way the service garage was leaning to one side, like a sad cartoon building. Trent eyed him a few seconds. A second message hit his phone and his thigh, bringing on the Pavlovian physical response he was starting to despise. "So, that's everything, I guess. You still think you can make a go of it, given how much competition there is for all this?" He raised his arms, indicating the twelve acres that had once contained the family business he'd so wanted to own himself someday. "Good luck to you."

Trent held out his hand. Noah shook it. "Thanks, Noah," the other man said. "Are you sure—"

Noah held up a hand. "Nope. I'm done with this. I have to be. I'm sorry. I know it's hard to understand."

"I think I get it." He smiled when they headed back to their cars, parked in the now weed-choked lot once teeming with business almost year-round. Their silence was awkward, but Noah didn't care. He wished he hadn't come here. It had only served to ramp up his general aggravation level. Even if he couldn't identify who he was more aggravated with—himself, Gayle, his shiftless, gambling-addicted father?

He sat behind the wheel of his truck, trying not to yell when the third text came through. With a loud sigh, he dragged the device from his pocket and stared at the screen.

Noah, I need help, she'd said about forty-five minutes ago.

Twenty minutes ago that became, *Please. I really need ur help. I know u r mad but I don't know who else to ask.*

Then, the final missive, *Please come help me.*

He stared at the words, marveling at how she could do this to him. At how badly he wanted to go to her, to help her with whatever it was. But he wouldn't. He couldn't. It was time to get real. Being around Gayle Connolly was the opposite of self-preservation. He had no control with her. He'd slip deeper into her world of money, spur-of-the-moment trips, of being a kid kept around for one reason and one reason only.

His dick shifted under his jeans, reminding him that particular reason wasn't so bad. "Down, boy," he commanded it, turning the key and putting the truck in reverse. As he drove away from the run-down buildings, still boasting the *Stokes* sign but with a *foreclosure auction* and a date sticker slapped over it, he realized too late he was driving toward downtown, toward Gayle.

He set his jaw and sped on the interstate, praying a cop would drag him down for speeding and break this spell she'd tossed over him, pulling her to him like a black widow spider. He chuckled. But it was not a happy sound, even to him. He exited without a speeding ticket and drove through the maze of downtown one-way streets on auto-pilot until he got to her building. And of course, there a super-convenient empty parking spot right in front of it. He sat, gripping the wheel and grinding his teeth for a few minutes, berating himself for coming here.

Finally, he got out, locked the truck and headed inside. The elevator held too many memories to be borne, so he ran up the steps, eager in spite of himself, happy, despite the many misgivings roiling in his brain, to at least lay eyes on her again. She opened the door from the stairwell before he could knock. He stood, hand raised, and looked at her. She had on a pair of well-worn jeans and a tight gray T-shirt emblazoned with the Fitzgerald label. Her mass of brown curls was yanked back in a ponytail and covered with a Tigers ball cap. Her face was devoid of makeup. Her smile was genuine and shot an arrow of something — part lust, part joy — straight into his chest.

"Hi," she said. "Thanks for coming."

He stood for a few more seconds, taking her in. When the fact she seemed to be wearing a pair of perfectly clean garden gloves covered in tiny flowers and was holding a similarly clean trowel registered, he grinned.

"I'm always up for gardening emergencies." He took a step into her kitchen, taking in the sights and smells he'd come to love about this place, and her. When he held out his hand, she put the spotless trowel into it with a sheepish grin. "What is the nature of your emergency, ma'am?"

"Out here," she said, turning and teasing him with her luscious rear view when she walked slowly to the open glass door onto her massive balcony. He'd said to her once that if she wanted, he'd set up some small gardens for her — flowers, cooking herbs, tomatoes. She'd laughed and claimed then he could but only if promised to maintain them. "I kill plants. They take one look at me and give up," she'd said.

"Wow," he said, impressed by the array of stuff she'd had delivered. Four long beds and three huge pots lay empty next to bags of soil and mulch. Trays of annuals, herbs and pots of decorative grasses—much of which he'd never have chosen for this spot since it didn't get enough direct sun during the day—were scattered all around. He touched each one, recalling their scientific names as he felt the various petals and leaves. He knelt down and inspected the pots and beds, noting with satisfaction that whoever had delivered them had lined them with pebbles for drainage.

When he rose, he stretched and closed his eyes in the midmorning sun, letting the happiness at this task and the company he'd be doing it in fill him from head to toe. "Okay then, green-thumb lady. Let's get to work." Without looking at her he grabbed a brand-new shovel and began cutting open the bags of soil. "Pour these in," he said, focusing on his task and not on how much he wanted to sweep her into his arms. "Fill each bed." He glanced around, mentally calculating the amount of soil needed and figuring she'd purchased enough.

They worked in companionable silence for almost thirty minutes while he opened the bags of soil and fertilizer, watching her struggling to pour them in without getting dirt all over the balcony's fake wood and concrete surface. After forty minutes, the beds were all prepped and ready.

"Jesus, this shit is hard."

He glanced over at her. Her pristine gloves were darkened with dirt. Her cheeks were smudged where she must have wiped sweat off her face. Several strands of dark curls had escaped both the hat and the tie-back and framed her face. She stood looking down at her handiwork. The sun was at its zenith, but it felt good, since the air temperature was a cool seventy degrees.

"You know, you're way late getting this done," he said, placing the small plastic potted flowers at intervals along the beds. He'd decided to use the big round pots for the grasses, so he could put them in some of the sunnier spots on the deck in hopes they'd survive the fall. "Most normal people had this finished eight weeks ago."

"Well, you know me. Bucking the trends is what I do." She stood over one of the large beds, trowel in hand, confusion on her face. "So, um, what do I do? Just dig a hole and stick these...things in it?"

He straightened from his task of dragging the big pots around and grinned at her. "You really are hopeless at this, aren't you? Here, let me show you."

She handed him the trowel.

"No, no, you hold it. Just crouch down and I'll guide you. You can't be an adult much longer without this skill, I don't think."

She smiled and crouched. He got behind her, instantly regretting it when the smell of her skin, combined with the fresh dirt and flowers, filled his nose, making him dizzy with desire. He took her hand and plunged the small shovel into the rich, black dirt, pulling out a plug of it just big enough for the small root system of the flowers he'd placed there. He took her other hand. Together they pulled the flower free of its plastic, stuck it in the hole and filled it in. She leaned into him, the warm press of her body making his head spin as they did the same with the next four plants he'd placed for the bed.

"This looks a little bare," she said at one point, her voice breathless enough to let him know she liked being close as much as he did. Unable to resist, he dropped the shovel and slid his hands up under her shirt. She shifted so she was on her knees, leaning over the half-finished planting bed. Her breasts were bra-less—they usually were when she was at home—and the familiar contours of them, the way her small nipples got rock hard under his fingers, made his dick rigid and aching under his zipper.

"My hands are dirty," he gasped when she pressed back into his crotch while he teased her breasts and lowered his lips to her neck. "Oh Christ, Gayle," he moaned. "I have missed you."

"Get me dirty, Noah," she whispered, reaching back to stroke his erection under his jeans. "Do whatever you want to me."

He fumbled with his button and zipper while she did the same. "Are you ready for me now, Gayle?" He reached down to yank slide her panties aside. "I'm serious, my hands are really dirty."

She reached back and grabbed his neck, angling her hips the way they'd found worked best when snagging a quick fuck in a beer cooler or her office. "Do it," she insisted. "Fuck me, Noah, right here. Right now. Oh Jesus, yes!"

He thrust deep, the tight glove of her pussy gripping him. "I'm gonna come," he growled. "I need to come inside you, Gayle."

She leaned forward, giving him a better angle. "You know I want it, Noah. Hurry. Give it to me."

He closed his eyes and dug his fingertips into her hips. As the orgasm burst across his brain, he let it take him, knowing this for a mere preamble to more fun later. She'd actually gotten him used to this method—coming fast and hard first, which allowed for a more languorous session later. It was fun, truth be told. Not holding back for an hour or more while providing pleasure to his partner had been one of things he looked forward to when they had sex. This wild urgency, the demands that he come, now, hard, within minutes of beginning had made him feel out of control at first, until she explained it was actually the opposite. It allowed him to maintain his control for hours afterward.

This particular climax was of the monstrous variety, since he'd been denying himself for over a week. He shivered and kept thrusting as she made soft, pleased noises that hit his ear like rose petals, or honeyed bourbon, or the silken touch of her sheets. He pulled out and sat back, still breathless while she pulled her jeans up and headed inside, returning a few minutes later with bottles of water. After managing to get himself back together, clothing-wise, he took one and drained it in two long gulps.

"Thanks," she said, gesturing around the still chaotic balcony.

"Don't thank me yet," he said with a wink. "We have hours left to do. I need to get to the store and find better options for these." He pointed to the large beds. "And you need better mulch. Plus…" He looked around. "We have to get some kind of irrigation set up. You've planted these things so late, they're gonna need a shit ton of water if you want them to survive into the fall."

She rolled her eyes. He smiled at her. "Bring it on, flower man," she said.

* * * *

"Dear God in heaven, I am sore as shit," Gayle said several hours later, rolling her shoulders and stretching

Liz Crowe

her arms up, giving him a delectable view of flesh between T-shirt and jeans.

"I told you." He was watering the large pots, thankful the builder had spared no expense for landscaping options. Whatever came from the bottom of each of their newly planted gardens headed right for well-placed drainage holes, which he assumed kept the balconies underneath from getting drenched. She wrapped her arms around him from behind, pressing her bra-less breasts against his back and running her hands up his shirt. "Better cut that out or we'll give the neighbors another show."

"I like giving shows," she said, lifting his shirt up and off while he shifted the hose from hand to hand to accommodate her. "Let's take a bath."

"Hang on. You can't just leave these plants without...whoa, there, okay. Hang on a sec." She'd popped the button on his jeans and unzipped him so fast he almost fell over. When he turned, he saw she was already stark naked right out here on her balcony. "Jesus, Gayle." He looked around, holding his T-shirt in front of her. "What are you doing?"

"The angle of this balcony means no one can see us, silly." She crooked her finger at him. "Come on. Time for a little clean up."

He grinned, shed his jeans and underwear and followed her across the living room and into her bathroom, where she already had the massive tub filling, candles lit and beer poured. "Nice setup. If I didn't know better, I'd think you were trying to seduce me." He pulled her close and kissed her, drowning in her the way only she could make him do with her delicious mouth and perfect body.

She broke away and pulled him to the tub. "Wait, let me shower off first." He jumped under the huge, rain-style shower head and let the side nozzles hit him from all directions. "Come on in." He pointed to her breasts, which were still smudged with dirt where he'd been fondling them earlier.

She ducked into the spray with him and let him soap her all over, paying special attention to her more sensitive parts. Once he deemed them clean, he turned off the water and pulled her to the tub, holding her hand for her to step into the hot, lightly bubbling water. She leaned back, sighing with satisfaction, which made his already eager dick even harder.

He got in, doing his own satisfied sighing at the sensation of the warm, lightly oiled water closing in around him. The tub was easily big enough for four people so he moved across from her, pulling her legs over his hips and watching her when he slid his hands up her thighs. He was doing it again, of course. He was substituting sex for actual communication. But right then, he didn't give two shits. He wanted to make her come, hard, more than once.

"Gayle," he murmured, moving his hands higher.

"Hmmm…" She kept her eyes closed when he stroked her clit and slid his fingers inside her, relishing the squeeze of her pussy. Her skin flushed red and her breathing quickened. He was damn proud of his hand and mouth skills when it came to pleasing women and he'd treated this woman to all of them, lots of times. The best orgasms weren't the quickies — the first ones they used to get themselves ready for more. No, these were the best. The slow, easy, almost lazy ones they'd work their way up to, retreat from, then ease close to again.

"Noah," she sighed, propping one of her legs up on the side of the tub. "Oh…baby."

"Touch your nipples, Gayle. Pinch them the way you like."

She cupped her breasts and began to tease her nipples. Her hips moved under the water as he teased and stroked and talked dirty to her until she cried out his name and grabbed his flexed biceps, gripping hard with the force of her climax. When she opened her eyes, they were so dark it was like staring into deep forest pools. "I…I…I love you."

Frowning, he rose from the water, his dick rigid, the water sluicing off his body. She stared up him.

"Don't say that. Not if you don't mean it." He stepped out onto the plush bath mat and pulled a towel off the warming rack. He was twanging with urgency. The compulsion to be inside her was so great it made his whole body ache. But he wasn't going to be played like this. He couldn't spare the emotional energy it would require.

He dried off and wrapped the towel around his waist, noting his cock was still at the ready as he headed into the bedroom. The kitchen beckoned, reminding him he hadn't eaten since early that morning, so by way of refocusing his energy, he rummaged around and found the ingredients for omelets and toast. Chopping onions, herbs from the newly planted gardens, green peppers and spinach eased his anger. He got the vegetables frying in the large ceramic pan, whipped the eggs until they were frothy then hit the down button on the toaster. Once he had the stuff in the skillet at the right point, he flipped everything over, using a quick jerk of his wrist, then sprinkled some goat cheese over half of it before folding it and sliding it out onto a plate.

Toast buttered, tomatoes sliced, omelet ready, he turned, knowing she was standing there. He could sense her comings and goings in a way that made him both pleased and a little nervous. Their connection ran deep, but he'd given up on calling it love weeks ago.

She took her plate and sat next to him on the tall chairs at the raised granite counter. "Thanks. I'm pretty famished."

He nodded, sipped water and ate, unwilling to break his silence yet.

The silky short robe she had on slipped off one shoulder. He turned to stare at her exposed flesh, his head thrumming with something he thought could be anger, if he let it. "I won't be anything but your equal, Gayle. This isn't about me playing with you. This about me…loving you with everything I have. I don't…" His voice broke. He cleared his throat. "I don't know if you're ready for it though. So I think I should probably leave." He got off the chair, rinsed his dishes and put them in the washer. While he washed the pan, bowl, whisk, knife and cutting board she continued to eat, not contradicting him, which told him all he needed to know.

He found his jeans and shirt on the balcony and put them back on before adjusting the timer on the weeping water hoses he'd bought with a better mix of decorative plants to get her through the fall. When he ducked back into the room, eyes adjusting from the bright light, he saw she was in the middle of the living room, stark naked and holding a large envelope.

"Stop it, Gayle," he said, giving her a wide berth on his way to the elevator doors. His heart felt as if it were breaking in a million pieces, but he knew it would only be worse if he allowed himself to do this, to let her pretend with him until she got tired of him. His own sense of self-worth had been battered for too many years to think otherwise.

"Noah, please. Wait." He turned to face her. "Here. This is for you." She held out the envelope. "I...I've been working on this for a while. It's the only way I know to prove to you how much I care about..." She closed her eyes and took a long breath. "How much I love you, okay? Do you have any idea how hard this is for me?"

Frowning, he took the envelope, undid the clasp and pulled out the papers inside. After studying them a few seconds, his trembling fingers let them drop to the floor. "*You* bought the landscaping business."

"Yes. I did." She didn't attempt to cover herself. No, his Gayle was nothing if not a pure exhibitionist. She'd loved showing off her body, showing off his and theirs as they'd made love or fucked their way through the past several weeks together. He fell back onto the nearest chair and put his hand over his face.

"You deeded it..."

"To you," she said. She was standing over him now. He could tell without looking. She took his hand and pulled him forward. Unable to stop himself, he wrapped his arms around her waist and pressed his face into her belly. She stroked his hair as he held on, riding wave after wave of emotion.

It was Gayle being Gayle, showing off and tossing her money around. The whole thing with Hettinger must have been a decoy, a way to get him mentally re-engaged while she'd gone and purchased it. And now, his family's company was his. The twelve acres and their decrepit buildings, the rusty equipment, the overgrown greenhouses.

Holy. Fucking. Shit.

He shoved her away. "How in the name of God do you think I can do this? I barely have two nickels to rub together and you know that. I can't afford to put it right, to get it going again. What in the hell am I supposed to do—"

She put her fingers to his lips. "It's all right. Trent's gotten some investors together on your behalf. I wasn't even involved in that part. As long as you, Noah Stokes, are in charge of the business again, there will be money to put it right. And not my money either." She smiled and cupped his cheek.

He was twanging and edgy, so he got up to pace, his mind wrapping around this new reality. "Investors," he said, dragging his fingers through his hair. "So I have to provide them with…"

"Profit, which no one doubts you will, once you have time and money to get things going again."

He froze in place, stunned by the enormity of this thing she'd done. "I…I need some air." He headed for the elevator, turning at the last minute to stare at her. "I love you, Gayle. I think I've loved you from the first time I saw you. But I don't know…I don't know about this."

"I love you too, Noah. And whether we stay together or not, Stokes Landscaping is yours again. Yes, I did it. But I did it for you."

He hit the button and stumbled into the lift, not meeting her eyes until the doors shut. He drove back out to the country and parked his truck in front of the doors of the old retail store. Guts churning, he got out and stared at it for what felt like hours.

Chapter Twenty-One

"Gayle?"

"What? Oh, sorry, Susan. I was drifting."

Her assistant smiled and pointed to her tablet.

"Right. Got it. So, tell me who I have to yell at today."

Gayle listened with half an ear, the rest of her checked out, as always, focused on what was missing from her life. Once her Friday afternoon debriefing was over, she shut the door behind Susan and flopped into her desk chair, furious with herself over her new-found inability to pay attention to anything but the fact Noah wouldn't return her calls or text messages or emails.

It had been three weeks since the weekend she'd presented him with her surprise. And while, if faced with the same opportunity again, she'd make the same decision about how to spend that particular amount of money, part of her wondered if buying the damn business back and deeding it over to him had been worst mistake of her life. She sighed and stretched, sensing the neglect and angst roiling through her, suffusing her nerve endings.

When a text made her phone buzz its way off the edge of her desk to the floor, she figured it was something else related to the fires she'd been putting out this week and ignored it. It wasn't until she made it all the way home and was sitting on her balcony, admiring how beautiful the flower beds had gotten by now, that she recalled it. She opened a beer on her way to her purse and took both phone and brew back outside with her to enjoy the waning moments of the Friday evening. A crispness edged the air, a sure sign of fall in Michigan.

She sipped and powered up her screen, staring down at the message until her eyes burned.

I'm in a dancing mood tonight. Meet me at Nexus at ten thirty. The usual table.

She bolted up, spilling half her beer down her front and dropping the phone onto the concrete. "Shit, shit, shit," she muttered, fumbling for the thing. It was already seven-thirty, and she'd need a shower, a bath, something. Her heart pounded in her ears when she tapped out a reply.

I'll be there.

She waited for a few minutes but didn't get a response. Praying she wasn't too late, she ducked into the shower, her skin tingling with anticipation. After the shower, she tried to close her eyes and relax, but could only accomplish it after rubbing out a quick orgasm. As she lay gasping and staring at the ceiling, she could only think of one thing, one name, one man.

Noah. He wanted to see her. *Thank God.*

At ten-forty she walked into the club and headed upstairs for their table. He was already there, as usual, sipping a beer and looking edible, as usual. His smile was wide, his hair a little long, his face tan from being outdoors—the way he loved, she knew. Which had been the whole reason behind her action to get him back to what he loved doing.

Knees shaking, she sat and took the frosty glass of straight Russian vodka he poured for her. They sipped while the sea of partying humanity surged around them, cocooning them, isolating them. Deciding she had to make the first move, she moved to the seat between them and put her lips near his ear. Everything she'd come to associate with him, that was so quintessentially Noah to her, filled her senses — leather, grass, dirt, but also a clean soapiness barely covered the smell of his skin. She touched her tongue to his earlobe, making him shiver. "I missed you," she said, before pulling away.

He rose, his incredible perfection filling her vision. He held out a hand. "Let's dance." She put her palm in his and let him pull her up. They stood, bodies pressed together, lips close but not quite touching. "I love you," she said, unable to think of anything else.

He nodded, turned and led her down to the dance floor. When he faced her, his expression was neutral. They stood among the gyrating crush of humanity until the music settled into her soul and she started moving. They danced for an hour, drank some water then danced more. He seemed to be having such a good time, she didn't ever want to stop. But after the second hour spent pretending to have sex, she wanted the real thing. She needed it. She wanted nothing more than to look into his eyes when he entered her body and tell him over and over again how much she loved him.

He pulled her close, his hand on her ass, his other one twined in hers. "Ready for the real thing, hot stuff?" His breath was hot on her ear. She nodded, on the ragged edge of orgasm already, with his thigh pressed against her clit. He dragged her back upstairs, grabbed the vodka bottle and they headed for the private rooms. Part of her didn't want it this way. She wanted her bed, or his. Their space, not this teeming building, with people all around them, many probably watching. But her body urged her forward, his delectable rear view in tight jeans making her rev even higher.

When they found their preferred room, he yanked the curtain shut, opened the bottle and took a long drink. Shivering with need, she reached for it, downed a portion then set it on the floor. Before she rose all the way up, he had her scooped into his arms, pressed down on the daybed, his hand up her skirt, his lips all over her neck and shoulders. She came fast, as usual, then reached for his zipper. "Wait," he insisted. "Just wait."

"You want inside me as bad as I want you there, Noah." His dark eyes blazed with lust. "Let's make us both happy, okay? Isn't that what all this is about?" Her chest was heaving but tears threatened even as she let him press her against the wall, lift one of her legs and thrust hard into her without preamble. "Oh. My. God. Yes!" She yelped with every thrust, gripping his shoulders and feeling him deep in her body, his pubic bone grinding against her clit.

"Gayle," he whispered, pounding into her. "Gayle. Gayle…"

"Yes, baby. Do it. I'm gonna…oh shit…" Her third orgasm of the day got serious and rolled up her spine, bursting across her vision as her body held his. He groaned into her neck and came with her, their cries drowned out in all the various yells, laughter and other people having sex all around them.

He pulled out of her fast and her feet hit the floor. When she nearly toppled over, he held her arm, but let go when she got her equilibrium back. He handed her tissues which she used between her legs, then tossed in the garbage. "Noah," she said, putting a hand on his shoulder while he zipped back up and tugged his sweaty shirt down. "Honey."

He turned to her, eyes blazing with anger. "Don't call me that. I'm not your goddamned honey. I'm your personal stripper, your gigolo, the boy you buy things for to keep him placated. Stop pretending it's anything else."

"What?" Her own anger rose, matching his. As if sensing it, he pressed her against the wall again, looming over her, his hand keeping her wrists pinned over her head. "Noah, you're hurting me."

"No, I'm not. I could. But I'm not." He sighed and let go of her. When her arms were freed, she put them around his neck. "Don't fuck with me, Gayle. I'm serious."

"Noah, I love you. I don't know how I can convince you that's true."

"You love Ethan. You only tolerate me."

Her chest tightened and words flew out of her mouth before she could stop them. "Fuck you!" The stridency of her voice surprised her. He blinked in the face of it. "No, really. Fuck you and the self-righteous horse you rode in on. I did love him. But I love you now, god damn it. Get out of my way." She tried to push him, but he was a wall of muscle and sinew. She sighed and let her hands drop to her sides. "I do love you, Noah. And I never, ever, *ever* thought I'd say that again."

He lifted her chin. The look in his eyes was the one she'd shied away from weeks ago but now welcomed and would cherish forever. Tears spilled down her cheeks.

"I…don't want you to cry anymore," he said, swiping at face with both thumbs. "Please, Gayle. Stop crying."

She pressed her face into his chest, sucking in deep breaths of him, her mind saying *Ethan, I love you. But I'm going now.*

He held her tight, the party going on around them. Finally, she pulled away and took his face between her hands. "I can't promise never to cry, but I do promise you that I love you, Noah Stokes."

He took her hands, kissed her knuckles then kissed her until her head swam and her body was tense with need. He gasped when he stopped but held her so she didn't slip to the floor, boneless with relief, lust, and happiness. "Can we go home?" she asked.

"Yes," he said, running his thumb over her lips. "We can go home."

Chapter Twenty-Two

One year later

"I don't know about you, but I'm ready for a beer. Noah? Gayle?" Austin pointed to them. He had his baby son strapped to his chest which was, Evelyn claimed, the only way the kid made it through the evenings without turning into a screaming hellion.

"Yeah, thanks. IPAs all around," Noah said, his fingers linked in hers. It had taken her a bit of time to get used to being half of a couple again. And not because of their age difference, which wasn't as great as the one between her and Ethan but, reversed, had a different cultural dynamic. She'd come to accept all her friends saw Noah as her equal, the way she did, so she could relax in social settings, like this one – the annual Fitzgerald Brewing Labor Day picnic. They always invited the TriCities staff to their massive house every year for it, where the food and beer flowed all afternoon and evening and into the night.

No one drove home from this event. She and Evelyn had arranged for a phalanx of car shares and taxis to be at the ready, and anyone who attempted to get behind the wheel drunk would have their keys snatched by a bunch of sober guys who'd been paid to patrol for that very thing.

She sat by the pool chatting with Ross and Elle Hoffman, the two brewers who'd met while working at Fitzgerald and now ran a trendy, successful restaurant in Detroit. Trent lounged nearby with his wife, Melody. His teenaged daughter from an earlier marriage sat holding her new sibling, giving her parents a break from baby duty. Noah must have gotten waylaid at the bar, likely talking about growing seasons, dirt, water — whatever. She smiled to herself at the thought of him, of them, of their life together, even though she worried almost constantly about being so ecstatic, figuring it would only get snatched away from her, like it had before.

"Here you go." Noah handed her a clear plastic cup full of Fitzgerald's finest IPA, interrupting her mild panic attack. He sat next to her, his arm draped over her shoulder, while people kept coming up to him to ask about the landscaping company and its new-found success. He'd hired a marketing and PR person who'd ramped things into high gear using social media and a 'Flower Man Blog', something Gayle was pretty proud of herself for initiating. It didn't hurt that the new owner of the old Stokes Landscaping Company was model-hot and not at all camera-shy. She put a hand on his leg, still shaky from their quickie in the shower before they'd come over. It had been a bit of a make-up encounter, after a long argument the night before.

She was getting obsessed about kids again—but not over wanting one. She knew it was unlikely, given how hard it had been the first time and the difficult labor that had produced her son. Every doctor had said she'd be unlikely to conceive again so after their first, unprotected hook-up they'd had all the tests for all the nasties and had compared healthy results over a hundred-dollar bottle of wine in their earliest, sex-drenched months and had declared themselves condom-free.

No, now her obsession was over the fact that Noah was saddling himself with a woman who simply didn't want, or more likely couldn't have, his child, even after he'd made it crystal clear he was sick of hearing about it. He'd never wanted kids. His passel of nieces of nephews had cured him of anything resembling baby lust, especially since some of them were approaching their teenaged years with a vengeance, driving his sisters crazy with their antics.

She sat back on the lounge and propped her feet on Noah's lap while he chatted and mildly flirted with a few of the bolder women who approached. She didn't care. Hell, she admired any woman who'd come right up and do her mating dance while he had his hand on her bare calves. She wasn't jealous in the slightest. He was hers. She was his. They were allowed to talk, even lightly flirt, with other people, as the situation required.

But she had her doubts about his loud protests regarding kids. Sighing, she looked around and motioned for Evelyn to come sit next to her. The place was getting busy, but her friend looked hollow-eyed and exhausted. "Hey, honey, will you get my friend a drink?" She poked Noah's firm thigh with her toe. "Pretty please?" She batted her eyelashes at him. He winked at her, which came damn close to having the power to make her climax lately.

"Things going well?" Evelyn asked, watching Noah make his way through the crowd.

"Perfectly, thanks." Gayle kept her gaze on his retreating ass, unable to stop staring at it.

"You guys gonna make it official sometime?"

"I don't know," she said, putting her empty cup on the table between them. "Maybe." She stretched, loving how sated and perfect she felt even as her body yearned for his proximity. She glanced up at Evelyn's house, wondering where she might corner him for a quickie later.

Evelyn smiled in a way that put Gayle immediately on edge. "What are you hiding from me?" she demanded, smacking her friend's arm.

"What? Nothing. Oh, thanks, Noah." Evelyn took her beer and winked at them before heading back into the crowd to play hostess with the most-est.

Gayle sighed and watched her friend go, gnawing on her bottom lip as the newly familiar baby-less worry hit her brain. Noah sat in Evelyn's abandoned chaise longue and stared at her.

"You're doing it again," he said, before downing his beer and pulling her into his lap.

"Doing what?"

He pressed his lips to her bare shoulder, making her shiver with happiness. Ever since she'd told Ethan she was 'going', the memories of him and her boy had begun to fade, not in an alarming way but in a completely appropriate one.

"You're making the Gayle face and that can only mean one thing."

She pulled away from and stared into his eyes. "Gayle face, huh?" She put her hand alongside his newly grown beard. "This is sexy, did I ever tell you?"

"Yeah, you did about an hour ago. Stop changing the subject."

"No, I'm serious." She rubbed her cheek along his, loving the rasp of the facial hair and recalling it between her thighs the night before. "I really like it."

"Gayle, cut it out." He thumbed her chin and met her gaze. "I told you a million times already, I don't want kids. Hell, it's like we're a perfectly matched couple that way, you know?"

She nodded.

"Stop it." He touched her chapped lip that she'd begun to worry with her teeth again. "I like this one too much for you to keep chewing on it." He kissed her softly, which did its usual number on her nerve endings. When he broke away, the noise of the party seemed to fade. "Stand up, woman. I need to do this the right way." She rose, her ears ringing. He pulled something from his pocket.

"Oh," she whispered when he opened a ring box, went down on one knee, and presented her with a lovely, vintage-looking diamond. "It was my great-grandmother's ring. I would be honored if you would wear it and marry me, Gayle."

She put a hand over her mouth. The infernal, ever-present tears rolled down her face. When she glanced over Noah's shoulder, she saw a crowd gathering, fronted by Evelyn, Austin, Melody, Trent, Ross, Elle, her mother and Helen, from the yoga studio. They were all smiling. When she realized she could see Ethan and Liam as clear as day, as if they were also standing in the happy, gathered group, she nodded to them.

"Go on, don't be a pussy," she could swear she heard her dead husband's bossy, profane voice demand. *"It's not like you. My Gayle goes for what she wants. Grab on and don't let go. Be happy, my darling. I love you."*

She closed her eyes. When she opened them, Ethan and Liam were gone, replaced by more clapping, laughing people who knew her, knew Noah and would support this crazy, fucked up thing she was about to do. "Yes," she said, her voice choked with emotion. "Yes. I will marry you."

He rose, slipped the ring on her finger and gathered her close. "I adore you, Gayle."

"I adore you too, Noah," she whispered. "But, um…" She glanced around as the crowd dissipated, headed back to the party.

"What is it, my love?" Noah asked, his lips hovering over hers again.

"I want to consummate this thing, like, now." She ran her hand down into his swim trunks and gripped his hardening cock. "You know? Like make it official and all?"

He grinned against her lips then kissed her and didn't stop until she broke away from him.

"I love you," she said, so unbelievably happy she honestly thought she might faint from it.

"I know," he said, taking her by the hand and leading her into the house, up the stairs and into his arms.

Want to see more from this author?
Here's a taster for you to enjoy!

FireBrew
Liz Crowe

Released 16ᵗʰ October 2018

Excerpt

"Are you sure this is the right space, Mister…ah…"

"Yeah." The very tall man in the reflective sunglasses grunted out his reply, ignoring my lapse with his name. Which was forgivable, considering he'd mumbled it to me on the phone before demanding to see my stale commercial listing, then hung up without giving me a half-second's chance to protest. Dropping everything and showing the old building that had once been home to a downtown Detroit fire station, which had languished for so long on the market it was collecting graffiti and wildlife, was not my idea of a great way to spend a warm Friday afternoon.

I had a hot date and this jerk was pissing me off the longer we stood shoulder-to-shoulder, staring at the once gleaming fireman's pole. I glanced at my phone, noting I now had exactly thirty-five minutes to do about an hour's worth of personal tidying up in order to make the seven p.m. deadline, for what I was determined would be a very satisfactory evening.

I shifted from foot to foot and waited the guy out, figuring him for yet one more porch-pisser—an out-of-towner, even—eager to snap some Instagram pictures and bemoan the death of a Great American City, historical building by historical building. These people loved their ruination porn. And I was one hundred percent not in the mood for it.

"Listen, Mister…"

"Trey," he said under his breath. He took yet another hike around the perimeter of the empty space. I watched him, admiring the rear view despite my anxiety about being late for the date with my shiny, new Internet-garnered friend whom I had every intention of benefiting from tonight. This guy claimed he'd just gotten off a plane and had driven straight down to the heart of what was once the old Irish neighborhood of Detroit—Corktown—just to see this stupid, echoing, useless and likely about to be condemned building. He looked the part of New York money—deep-blue suit, dazzling white shirt and blood-red tie. The sort of person who would buy a pile of shit like this and either raze it for condos or lovingly and expensively restore it—into condos.

He'd made it all the way across what I assumed was a former parking area for fire trucks when he whirled around, whipped off his glasses and pinned me with such a strange look I took a few steps back.

"I want it," he said clear as day, his voice low, raspy and firm. "But I'm not paying this." He shook the feature sheet he'd yanked out of my hands the second I'd met him at the door. His eyes were of the deepest, darkest brown. They matched his chestnut-colored hair, which was thick and wavy in a way that might make a girl jealous if she weren't inclined to plunge her fingers into it — like I was right then.

I opened my mouth to reply but my throat had closed up. Shaking my head to clear it, berating myself for thinking anything about the guy at all, much less entertaining the alarming porn loop running through my head starring us both, I tried again.

"All right, Mr. Trey, I'll have to — "

"No mister. Just Trey." He remained as far across the room from me as possible. "George Lattimer the Third. Trey, you know, for the third?"

"Ah, well," I said, resisting the urge to wipe the sweat off my upper lip, but only just barely. "Right. So…anyway," I blathered, pissed off at my own nervousness. "I have to take any offers, in writing, to the attorney for the estate holding the title. I assume you're — "

"Fifty-seven," he interrupted me. Again.

"You're joking," I blurted out, shifting into negotiation mode, no longer giving a shit he was the hottest thing on two male legs I'd encountered in, well, my entire life. He took a few corresponding steps away, looking like he was afraid I'd spray girl cooties on him if I got any closer. Up close, sans mister cool shades, those eyes were of the sort I might call mesmerizing — if I were the kind of person to think such a thing about some dude's eyes. "The list price is ninety-nine. I get the place is a little, um…"

"Shitty?" He leaned against the far wall, arms crossed, smirking at me. "Falling apart as we speak? No better than a rat hole?"

"It has some deferred maintenance issues, yes," I said, walking closer to him. He didn't move this time. "But I assure you that the seller — "

"Give him my offer," Trey said before turning away and wandering into the area that had once housed the kitchen and living spaces, leaving me standing, leaning forward and ready to engage—how exactly, I wasn't quite sure. I trotted after him, clickety-clacking in my stilettos across the concrete, doing all I could to avoid random clumps of God-knows-what detritus that multiplied every month the building sat here empty.

I found him in the farthest reaches of gloomy interior, near what I assumed used to be the storage for extra firemen suits and equipment. He stood at the open door, peering into the gloom. I took a minute to gather my thoughts and words, ignoring the perfect V-shape of his torso in its dark suit coat. I love a man in a suit. It's a known fact. But this guy was being a rude asshole, be-suited perfection be damned.

I tapped his shoulder, trying to make my touch firm, in command and take-no-prisoners. He turned so fast I flinched and stumbled backward, catching my heel on a ball of rags probably home to an entire family of rats. The expression on Trey's face was one of abject panic, as if I'd poked him in the side with a semi-automatic weapon, or maybe a tampon. I scrabbled around, hoping not to land on my ass in the filth, and he reached out and caught my flailing arm, his movements calm and practiced. In that instant, I acknowledged if he pulled me closer, I wouldn't protest.

I blew out a breath, settling myself back on top of my too-high heels. When he let go and stepped away, I felt rejected.

Ridiculous, I know. But I did.

"Wow, sorry," I said, tucking stray strands of hair behind my ears, looking anywhere but at him. "I'm usually not such a klutz, but you—"

"Give him my offer. He'll take it." The man's voice had natural certainty, but he was smoking meth if he thought the seller would take half his asking price. "Give him this," Trey said, holding out a business card.

I took it, wishing I could use it as an excuse to touch his fingers or something equally desperate. But he held it by one corner and unless I grabbed the man's hand, it would not be happening. I took it and glanced down without really reading it before I looked back up at him. "What do you want the place for anyway? You an investor or a builder?"

"Neither," he said, stuffing his hands into his trouser pockets. The silence spun out between us, visible, like the puffs of outside air sending tendrils of dust and other nastiness swirling around. I blew out another breath in frustration.

"Giving the whole 'strong and silent type' thing a real go, aren't ya?" Without allowing the man the satisfaction of my continued attention, I pulled out my phone and hit my seller's preprogrammed number. I just hoped I would have time to contact my date — *oh dear sweet Jesus, what's his name?* — and give him a heads up I'd be late, or we'd have to cancel.

Once I left the requisite message with the lawyer's service, I turned back around. Trey had resumed his perusal of whatever was in the storage area, so I resumed mine of his pleasant rear view. Long legs, no-doubt firm ass, skin bronzed. He must have been ex-military or maybe a cop — something that kept him outdoors for a lot of years — none of which squared with the suit.

"When will you get a response?" he asked, still facing away from me.

"Tomorrow. Now, if you'll excuse me, I have to — "

"Come to dinner with me," he said, shocking me to my toes. He turned to face me, his chocolate-colored gaze intense.

"No, thanks," I said, drawing myself up and getting huffy at his assumption. "You're a rude asshole, if you'll pardon me. Besides, I already have a date."

He tilted his head, giving me the oddest top-to-toe eyeballing. The corner of his full upper lip lifted in what might pass for a smile. "Cancel it," he said.

"Um, no, I don't think so," I said, my voice quaking in an annoying, uncharacteristic manner. I didn't back down when he stood way up in my personal space bubble, looking down at me as if I were the mouse between his furry cat paws. "You don't intimidate me, *George*," I said.

He chuckled. "Come on. I'm starving. Tell your boyfriend you have to take a big important client out to dinner." He raised a dark eyebrow, giving me a moment to ponder his possibilities.

"You don't know what you're getting into with me," I said, smiling, willing to play along, my body already reacting and knowing full well where this was going even if I was more than a little surprised by his rapid-fire change of mood.

"I think I just might, *Harriet*," he said, his smile widening.

"Jane, please," I said with an edge in my voice, using the middle designation I'd insisted on from the moment I realized my parents had saddled me with my great-grandmother's old-fashioned first name. How the man knew it was anyone's guess, but I decided not to ask him. "I have to go to my office first." He nodded but didn't say anything more.

For reasons completely unknown to me at the time, I sent my date-for-the-night a cancellation text, tucked my phone into my purse and accepted Trey's outstretched elbow.

About the Author

Amazon best-selling author, mom of three, Realtor, beer blogger, brewery marketing expert, and soccer fan, Liz Crowe is a Kentucky native and graduate of the University of Louisville currently living in Ann Arbor. She has decades of experience in sales and fund raising, plus an eight-year stint as a three-continent, ex-pat trailing spouse.

With stories set in the not-so-common worlds of breweries, on the soccer pitch, in successful real estate offices and at times in exotic locales like Istanbul, Turkey, her books are unique and told with a fresh voice. The Liz Crowe backlist has something for any reader seeking complex storylines with humor and complete casts of characters that will delight, frustrate and linger in the imagination long after the book is finished.

Don't ever ask her for anything "like a Budweiser" or risk bodily injury.

Liz loves to hear from readers. You can find her contact information, website details and author profile page at http://www.totallybound.com.